IT STARTED WITH A RESCUE

NANNY TALES: THE HAMPTONS, BOOK 1

JILLIAN ADAMS

JILLIANADAMS.COM

ONE

I took a deep breath of the salty sea air and released it with a happy sigh.

A few months ago, my life had been very different as I navigated through the last of my final exams and the anticipation of high school graduation. Instead of hearing the crash of waves against sun-warmed sand, I'd heard the slam of lockers and the excitement of my friends as they discussed their summer plans.

My only plans had been to help out at my grandfather's farm, cleaning out horse stalls and chasing the goats around.

That was, until my best friend Kelsie rescued me.

A seagull jetted across the sky, not far above me. I watched its wide wings spread as it sailed through the air. What could be better than spending the summer on an actual beach?

Wet sand smacked into my cheek, followed by a shrill shriek of laughter and another fistful of sand.

"Hey!" I gasped and narrowly dodged getting a mouthful of sand.

The four-year-old girl crouched in front of me shrieked with laughter again. Her chocolate brown curls bounced around her chubby cheeks as she readied another handful of sand.

"Cherish!" Kelsie huffed from beside me. "Now, sand is for building sand castles, not for throwing." She picked up the bucket half dug into the sand beside her and handed it over to her young charge.

As I wiped the sand from my cheek, I heard the infectious giggles of two-year-old Anthony beside me.

"Again!" He clapped his sand-covered hands.

"Thanks a lot, Anthony." I laughed as I covered his tiny feet with sand.

Maybe it wasn't exactly a tropical vacation but landing a job as a nanny in the Hamptons felt as foreign to me as seeing the wide expanse of the ocean stretched out before me.

Thanks to Kelsie's cousin being friends with two families in need of some summer help, we had both been given the opportunity to travel from our landlocked lives to an entirely different world—a world that came with toddlers and pre-schoolers, but a new world just the same.

"Jaxx, can you please stop Bella from chasing that bird?!"

I turned to see Hannah where she sat on a reclined beach chair beneath a wide umbrella just behind us.

"Absolutely, Hannah!" I jumped to my feet, a little embarrassed that I hadn't noticed that my four-year-old charge had been terrorizing a seagull.

Hannah Celeste—wife of Douglas Celeste, owner of a national chain of bakeries—was a beautiful woman. Her chestnut hair was always arranged perfectly around her face, and despite the summer heat, she hadn't sweated off a trace of her natural-looking make-up. She'd had two children, but her bikini revealed no hint of either pregnancy.

Seated on the beach chair beside her was Patti Collingsworth, mother to Cherish—Bella's best friend.

I scooped up Anthony in my arms as I chased after Bella, who continued to chase after the bird.

"Bella honey, we have to let the birdie be a birdie, it's not a toy!"

"Mine!" Bella screeched and lunged for the bird again.

I heard Kelsie's laughter not far behind me.

I rolled my eyes and tried again. "Bella! If you stop chasing the birdie, we can make a big sand castle!"

"We can?" She turned to face me with a wide smile and the giant blue eyes that she shared with her mother.

"Absolutely." I sighed with relief. I didn't have the natural talent with kids that Kelsie seemed to.

"But Anthony will smash it!" Bella put her hands on her hips.

"Smash!" Anthony giggled and struggled to get out of my grasp.

"I'll protect it." I guided her back to our spot in the sand and we teamed up with Cherish to work on the castle.

While Anthony began digging a hole in the sand, Kelsie leaned close to me.

"I overheard Hannah and Patti talking about taking the kids to get some lunch. I think we're going to get some time off soon."

"Great." I smiled at the thought. "Maybe we can go for a swim?"

"You can!" Kelsie tugged at her blonde hair, which she had wound into an elaborate braid. "This hair isn't going near that water."

"You knew we were coming to the beach; why did you spend so much time on it?" I squinted at her as the sun glared down on us.

"Oh, honey, this hair isn't for the beach, it's for him." She tipped her head toward the nearby lifeguard stand.

Perched atop the white wooden structure, dressed only in bright red swim trunks, was a golden-skinned guy with messy

3

light brown hair. The silver whistle that dangled from his neck rested against his broad chest.

"Ugh, a lifeguard?" I shook my head as I looked away from him. "Could you be any more predictable?"

"Oh, it's not just him. It's also him and him and that guy over there." She pointed out several other cute boys that dotted the beach. "I don't know what you plan to do with your summer, but I am going to enjoy every second of it, whether it's with a lifeguard or one of these other cuties. I'm not picky." She laughed. "That's your problem, Jaxx—you're too picky."

"Oh sure, *that's* my problem." I rolled my eyes as I tightened the ponytail I always wore my long dark hair in.

While Kelsie sported a bikini that showed off her spectacular figure, I wore a tankini, chosen so that I didn't need to worry about things slipping out of place while I swam or ran on the beach—two things I was definitely looking forward to doing this summer.

I didn't mind being in my swimsuit—it showed off my tanned skin and the lean muscle I'd built from years of playing sports in high school—but Kelsie and I couldn't be more different when it came to our figures. And usually, it was her type that the guys were attracted to. I'd accepted that, but admittedly I now found myself feeling just a bit out of place among the beautiful people in the Hamptons.

TWO

"You are too picky. It's the truth, Jaxx. If you let me get my hands on you for ten minutes, I could transform you into the hottest babe on this beach."

"Make-up and fashion can't fix everything, Kelsie." I laughed as I looked out over the water. I loved to swim back home, but I'd never swum in the ocean before. I dug my toes into the warm sand, eager to experience it for the first time. "I still can't believe we're here."

"Me either." Kelsie smiled. "We're going to have such a great summer and I'm so glad we're here together!" She gave me a quick hug.

"Let's go, kids!" Hannah called out. "We're going to have some lunch." She paused just behind me. "You two can have an hour to do what you please. Remember if you want any food from the club dining room just give them our names and it'll be put on our tab."

"Thanks so much." I got to my feet as Hannah gathered her sand-covered children. "Enjoy your lunch."

"I'll try." Hannah laughed as she brushed some sand off

Bella's legs. "Maybe we could leave some sand on the beach, kids?"

As they walked away, Kelsie waved her hand at me. "Jaxx, you're blocking my sun!"

"Sorry." I stepped to the side. "Did you use enough sunscreen?"

"We're here to have fun, remember?" Kelsie grinned up at me as she stretched out on her towel. "You're Bella's and Anthony's nanny, not mine!"

"Sorry." I held up my hands as I laughed.

She wasn't wrong; I did tend to be protective of her. Maybe it came from having a younger sister. Lucy, who was sixteen, often accused me of the same.

Kelsie fondly called me a nurturing soul, but I knew what she really meant. Sometimes I could be a little uptight. I didn't always relax and have fun like most other people my age— unless I was doing some type of sport. I always felt the most comfortable when I was active.

As I stared down at my beautiful friend, I felt a pang of envy. She definitely seemed to fit in here. Me, on the other hand? Well, I wasn't sure yet. Hopefully I wasn't totally sticking out like a sore thumb.

I glanced back at the ocean. "Are you sure you won't swim with me? Maybe just wade in the water?"

"Not now, I only have an hour to get that lifeguard to look away from the water long enough to notice me." She shifted on her towel and peered at me over the top of her sunglasses. "I plan to use every second."

"You do know he's supposed to look at the water?" I laughed. "What if someone needs saving?"

"I'm someone. I could use some saving." She shrugged, then pushed up her sunglasses and angled her face in the direction of the lifeguard stand.

I held back more laughter, then turned to face the water. If Kelsie didn't want to swim with me, I wouldn't let that hold me back. I tightened my ponytail, then ran toward the water's edge.

Already the strength of the ocean fascinated me. The sound of the waves as they crashed against the sand, the ripple of the water as it ran back from the shore—I'd never seen anything like it.

When my toes hit the cold water, I took a sharp breath in. Despite its being summer, the water was cooler than I expected. A shiver crept up my spine, but I continued forward. I never backed down from a challenge and trying something new was my favorite kind of challenge.

Confidence built within me as I walked out to my waist and prepared to dive in. Swimming I could do. I'd been on the swim team back home and had won a few competitions.

Before I could dive in, a wave slammed right into me. I gasped at the power of the water as it stung my skin and caused me to stumble back a few steps.

Flustered, I glanced over my shoulder to see if Kelsie had noticed.

While she seemed uninterested, I briefly caught the eye of the lifeguard perched on his stand. My heart pounded as I realized his eyes were locked on me. Why? Could he tell how inexperienced I was with this whole ocean scene?

I turned back to the water, determined not to let his attention distract me.

When the next wave crashed toward me, I faced it with more confidence. It still pushed me a bit, but I knew what to expect this time. As soon as it passed, I slipped under the water for a swim.

As the cool water engulfed my body, I felt the sensation of weightlessness that made swimming one of my favorite sports. I started to break through the surface to come up for air, but a wave knocked me right back under. As I tumbled through the water, I lost track of what was up and what was down.

For a brief moment I felt panic.

Then my toes hit the sand and I shoved myself upward.

This time, when I broke through the surface, I didn't get knocked back under. I gulped down a few breaths as I tried to get my bearings. A glance back at the beach revealed that I'd moved quite far away from Kelsie and I was now in water up to my neck.

Clearly, I had a lot to learn about swimming in the ocean.

I heard a shrill whistle and looked toward the lifeguard stand. The lifeguard waved his hand in the air.

I squinted at him, then glanced over at some other people in the water. It had to be them that he was whistling at. I wasn't doing anything wrong.

I shrugged it off and ducked back under the water, determined to master swimming in the ocean.

Once again, the weightless sensation relaxed me. I felt the tug of the current as the waves retreated but didn't pay much attention to it other than to figure out the timing of the next wave.

As I broke through the surface again for a breath, I glanced back toward the beach. This time, I had to squint to see Kelsie.

THREE

The sudden distance between myself and the beach left me breathless. And my toes couldn't find the sand beneath me.

"Calm down, Jaxx." I took a deep breath. "Just swim back to shore, it's no big deal."

I smiled at the thought of being able to use my swimming techniques.

As I stroked my arms through the water and swam back in the direction of the beach, I thought about one of my proudest moments. I felt my muscles flex and strain as my hands dug down through the water, just like they had during that race in my junior year.

It had been a mixed competition created by the swim teams —not sanctioned by the school, but something just for fun in a boys versus girls scenario. One of those boys happened to be the only real boyfriend I'd ever had.

Vincent.

The name played through my mind. I'd always considered it an old-fashioned name and I'd started calling him Vinny.

He liked that. He liked everything about me, it seemed, when he would call me all the time and insist that we spend time together. His demands annoyed me a little as they'd distracted me from my practice schedule, but Kelsie had assured me that it was normal for a boyfriend to want to spend time with his girlfriend.

Girlfriend.

That title still didn't seem right for what our relationship had been. Even the word relationship didn't seem right. We'd kissed a few times, argued many more times, and on our last day together, he had what I considered to be a total breakdown over the fact that I'd beat him—the strongest swimmer on the boys' team—in front of all his friends.

While I'd jumped up and down, basking in my victory with the girls from my swim team all around me, he'd glared at me from the pool.

I'd gone from elation and pride to a sense of dread. What had I done that was so wrong? Was I supposed to let him win?

I pushed the thought away as I continued to swim through the water.

None of that mattered now. Vincent was just a memory and my life was just beginning.

Still, no matter what I said to Kelsie, a small part of me longed for what she seemed to stumble into with every step—real romance, maybe even real love. But if my dating history had taught me anything, it was that I apparently didn't do that right.

I broke through the surface with a breath of air, ready to wave to Kelsie on the beach. To my surprise, the beach was even further away. My arms ached from how long and far I'd been swimming.

How was it possible that I had actually drifted further out?

My heart raced with uncertainty. Had I somehow gotten confused? Had I been swimming in the wrong direction? A few other swimmers were still a bit further out than me, but not many.

I squinted toward the horizon and gulped at what I thought might be a shark fin. Were there sharks in the Hamptons?

I had no idea. I didn't want to find out.

Despite the pain in my arms, I began to swim again, this time even faster. I was determined to get back to shore before I saw any large teeth gnashing in my direction. Worn out and ready to crawl back onto the sand, I surfaced, eager to see the shore just steps away.

Instead, my toes sloshed through open water and I couldn't even tell where Kelsie was on the beach. Confused and frustrated, I started to feel some fear surface inside of me.

What if I couldn't get back? What if no one noticed I was gone?

I looked toward the faint image of the white lifeguard stand. As I peered at it, I was almost certain that there was no one in it. My heart began to pound even harder.

What kind of lifeguard left his post?

If he'd been there, I might have waved my hands for help, as embarrassing as that would have been. Instead, it was clear that I was completely on my own.

My body felt heavy as I tried to swim again. The weightlessness of the water didn't feel peaceful now. Instead, it made me panic even more. With the tug of the current I could easily be swept away.

I looked around for any other swimmers nearby that might be able to help me. My chest tightened as I realized that I was further out than any other person in the water.

"The worst thing you can do is panic, Jaxx." My own voice sounded foreign to my ears, maybe because of the fear in it.

I just had to get back to the beach. I knew how to swim. I'd swum hundreds of hours. I'd won competitions. I'd beaten Vincent. Of course I could get back to the shore. I just had to try harder.

With a determined chant playing through my mind I started to swim again.

In the distance ahead of me, I could see someone swimming.

Eager to get the person's attention, I waved my hands through the air. Just at that moment, a large wave—one I didn't expect as far out as I was—crashed right over me. Its strength pushed me down under the water and spun me around. I felt bits of sharp shells strike my skin, rocks graze my feet, and water rush into my nostrils. As the churn of the water threatened to spin me again, I felt something else—something rock solid and warm, as it wrapped around my waist.

Jerked upward, I panicked and fought against whatever had a hold of me.

The grasp tightened and soon I broke through the surface of the water.

Desperate for air, I gasped as I sprawled heavily against a tanned chest with the whistle worn around his neck pinned between us.

FOUR

"You." I stammered out the word as he kept me pinned against him.

"Don't try to talk. You must be exhausted. I'll get us back to the shore." He slid the red buoy under my arms and guided me to rest on it.

As I clung to it, I felt my cheeks burn with embarrassment. My first day at the beach and the lifeguard had to jump in to rescue me. Not only that, but he made short work of swimming us both back to the shore.

As we neared the water's edge, Kelsie jumped to her feet. "Jaxx!"

"Easy now." The lifeguard helped me through the rough surf at the edge of the sand until I was on dry land again. "I saw how hard you were working out there." He paused as he looked into my eyes. "Didn't you hear me whistle? I tried to get your attention before you got too far out."

"I'm sorry about all of this." My chest ached as I looked away from his dark green eyes. "I'm really a strong swimmer—I don't know what happened out there. Every time I tried to swim back to shore, I seemed to get further out."

"The currents can be tricky." He tilted his head to the side as he swept his wet brown hair away from his forehead. "Is it your first time in the ocean?"

"Yes." I sighed as Kelsie put her hands on her hips. "I was really excited to go for a swim."

"It's always best to swim parallel to the shore." He held out his arm to show me. "You'll think it's best to swim straight back in, but if the currents are strong, you can't overcome them. When you swim parallel you can get out of the current and then swim in." He looked straight into my eyes. "Are you sure you're okay? I can take you to get checked out if you want."

"I'm fine, thank you." I could barely even look at him as I felt my cheeks growing hotter and hotter. How had I managed to embarrass myself so badly on my first day at this fancy beach? "And thanks so much for your help."

"That's what I'm here for." He smiled as he glanced over at Kelsie, then looked back at me. "You're working for the Celestes, right? I saw you with them earlier."

"Yes. Just for the summer. And my friend Kelsie works for the Collingsworths." I gestured for her to come over.

"Good you have a friend with you." He nodded to Kelsie, then looked back at me. "I'm Nate, by the way. Jaxx, is it?" He raised his eyebrows.

"Creative parents." I grinned, then nodded.

"Cool name." He grinned back at me.

"Thanks for being there to save her!" Kelsie lifted her sunglasses and smiled at him. "Jaxx is such a troublemaker."

"I am not!" I laughed.

"Glad I could help." Nate met Kelsie's eyes. "Make sure she takes it easy for a little while. She had quite a scare." He looked back at me and held my gaze for a long moment. "You're sure you're okay?"

"I'm fine." I shrugged. "Just slightly mortified."

"Girls!" Hannah waved from the clubhouse. "Time to pack up! The kids definitely need their naps."

"Right away!" I held my breath as I wondered if she had seen me being rescued. I hoped not too many people had. When I turned back to thank Nate again, he'd already climbed back up onto the lifeguard stand.

I started gathering the sand toys, my heart still pounding from the entire experience.

"Wow, does he have a thing for you!" Kelsie squealed as she folded up one of the blankets.

"What?" I looked over at her with a laugh.

"Oh please, don't tell me you couldn't see how he was fawning over you!" She shook some sand from another blanket.

"Kelsie! He literally saved my life." Those words hit me hard. I had been exhausted by the time he'd gotten to me. What if he hadn't noticed that I was in trouble? I glanced back in his direction and saw another lifeguard in the stand. Shorter, with short blond hair and a deeper tan, he didn't look anything like Nate. "You're being ridiculous." I grabbed the last shovel out of the sand. "A guy like him would never be interested in someone like me."

"Now you're the one that's being ridiculous!" Kelsie rolled her eyes. "You have no idea how beautiful you are!"

I did my best to ignore her words. Kelsie always made an effort to be a good friend and try to build me up, but I knew the truth, I simply wasn't her. If Nate was interested in anybody, it would definitely be Kelsie.

"Are you two free tonight?" He spoke up from just behind me.

I spun around, so startled that I nearly knocked into him. "What?"

"Depends on what you have in mind." Kelsie grinned as she picked up the last blanket.

"A few of us get together to play volleyball around six. It's just a friendly game. I thought you two might like to join us," he answered Kelsie and then his eyes met mine.

"Oh, I have to work through dinner." I took a step back and nearly dumped my bucket of toys.

"Come after." He smiled.

"Like I said, I'll be working." I forced a smile in return, then walked across the sand toward Hannah.

When Kelsie caught up with me, she elbowed me in the side. "What was that?"

"What?"

"You just left him hanging." She groaned. "He wants to spend time with you."

"You're nuts, Kelsie. If anything, he was hoping that you would say yes."

"Uh-huh, because I'm the one he was staring at." She shook her head, then chased after Cherish.

I looked back toward the beach, but if Nate was still there, the crowd had swallowed him up.

Seconds later, two little munchkins were demanding all my attention again.

FIVE

As I prepared dinner for the kids, I couldn't keep my mind off what had happened to me that day. Thank God, Nate had been there to pull me to shore. Really, it all could have ended very badly. It was good to know that the lifeguards here were taking their jobs seriously—that they weren't just good to look at. Good grief! I cringed. Where had that come from?

"Peas!" Bella groaned as she poked at the green balls on her plate. "Why?"

"Because they're good for you." Hannah laughed as she put together a plate of food for herself. "Jaxx, please help yourself, I don't want you going hungry."

"Thanks." I smiled at Bella as I added a big helping of peas to my plate. "These will be delicious. I'm going to eat them all!"

"All of them?" Bella squeaked as her eyes widened.

"Yup!" I popped one into my mouth. "Tasty!"

Bella stared at me, then picked up one of her peas and popped it into her mouth. "Yuck!" She moaned.

"Oh, Bella, just eat them." Hannah huffed. "You know you only get dessert if you eat your dinner."

Bella stuck out her bottom lip then began pushing the peas around on her plate.

"Did you get to go for a swim today, Jaxx?" Hannah took a bite of her chicken.

I felt my cheeks grow hot. "Yes, I did. It was my first time in the ocean."

"Oh. I didn't realize that." Hannah frowned. "How did you like it? I know it can be a little scary for some people."

"It was a little scary, actually—but, in the end, I enjoyed it."

Was that even a true statement? Well, I would enjoy it next time, anyway.

"Good. I love my time at the beach, but I'm not a huge fan of being in the water." She continued to chat about the day and the plans for the summer.

I appreciated how friendly she was with me and I tried to concentrate on her words, but my thoughts kept traveling right back to Nate. He'd seen me. He'd noticed me struggling. If it wasn't for him, maybe I wouldn't have made it back in. The thought shocked me.

Bella's sweet voice brought me out of my wandering thoughts.

"I ate all of them!" She grinned as she scooted her plate in my direction.

"Great job, Bella!" I smiled at her as I picked up her empty plate.

"Daddy's going to let me have ice cream!" Bella sung out as she jumped down from the table.

"Yum!" Anthony giggled as he smacked his hand against his high chair tray, which still had a bit of his dinner smashed on it.

"Oh, that's right, Jaxx, I forgot to tell you." Hannah took the plate from me, then handed me a washcloth for Anthony's tray. "Douglas is going to be home early tonight and the four of us are going to watch a movie and have ice cream. You're welcome to join us, but I'm sure there are more fun things for you to be doing." Her eyes sparkled as she looked at me. "I remember my summers here when I was your age. So, feel free to go out for the evening."

"Oh wow, are you sure?" I wiped off Anthony's tray, then set him free from his high chair.

"Of course. I want you to have fun while you're here. You being here lets me have some kid-free time, which is a huge luxury, so anything I can do to make sure you're having a good time too—I want to do that." She glanced toward the front door as it swung open.

"There he is now!"

"Daddy!" Both kids squealed as they ran for the tall man who filled the doorway.

"Ah! Wild animals!" Douglas laughed as he held up his briefcase to protect himself.

I smiled as I watched him. Already I loved being around the Celestes. Seeing Bella and Anthony fight over hugging their father inspired a pang of homesickness for my sister.

Hannah was right, I needed to get out and have some fun, and volleyball was one of my favorite sports. I'd never gotten to play on a real beach before. The thrill of sending the ball flying across the net always got my blood pumping.

I called Kelsie to see if she could join me.

"Sorry, I'm stuck here for another hour. Patti and Tucker like to have a kid-free dinner together, so it's a show and then a bath for Cherish while they eat. But I can meet up with you later." She paused. "Wait, are you going to the volleyball game?"

"I was thinking about it." I bit into my bottom lip.

"You should!" She nearly shouted. "Oh, Nate is going to be so happy you're there!"

"Kelsie, enough with the Nate stuff, okay?" I laughed. "I

just want to play some volleyball. Who knows if they'll even still be out there? It is almost sunset."

"Go. You have to go. Just trust me on this, Jaxx. Just show up. What can it hurt?"

"You're right. I'll see you later." I took a deep breath, then hung up the phone.

After everything that had happened that day, something physical was exactly what I needed. Plus, a part of me felt that I needed to redeem myself in Nate's eyes—show him that I wasn't totally incompetent when it came to using my strength. As strong as his arms were, I guessed that he could spike the ball almost as well as me. And now, I was definitely up for the challenge!

SIX

As I walked across the street in the direction of the beach club, I really hoped that the game was still going. It seemed like it might be exactly what I needed to rid my body of the stress that I still felt from earlier.

As I neared the beach, I noticed the volleyball net a little further down. I could see people still playing, but the game had already started. I couldn't just break into it. I'd arrived too late. Still, the draw of the beach and the warm breeze was enough to get me out on the sand.

I walked past the net, my eyes on the shells that had washed up in the sand.

As the frothy water lapped at my toes, I felt a little disappointed. Maybe if I'd arrived earlier, I would be playing volleyball with the others. Now I just felt awkward as I looked out over the water and wondered why I'd bothered at all. When it came to playing a sport with a guy, I had no trouble. I knew my role, and how to play it. But when it came to anything else, I felt absolutely lost.

"Jaxx!"

My muscles tensed as I recognized his voice and realized he

was only a few steps away from me. I turned and saw him crossing the last of the distance between us.

"I thought that was you." He smiled as his eyes settled on mine. "I'd know that ponytail anywhere."

"Really?" I laughed as I flicked it over my shoulder. "I guess I'm a little too late for the game."

"Yeah, it's breaking up." He glanced back toward the group of people that had begun to scatter in different directions. "Usually we finish up before the sun actually sets." He looked up at the sky, then back at me. "The beautiful sunset is too much of a distraction."

I smiled at his words.

When Kelsie had pointed him out on the lifeguard stand, I had assumed some things about him. I'd assumed that he was far too hot to care about much other than beautiful tanned blondes and that his level of intelligence extended about as far as the tip of his nose. In my experience, most guys his age—and with his looks—were only interested in a few things and they certainly didn't consider the sunset distracting.

"It's stunning." I nodded as I began to walk along the water again. I was sure he had somewhere else to be.

"How do you like it here so far?" He matched his pace to mine.

"It's gorgeous." I smiled. "I'm really glad I'm here. I'm looking forward to the rest of the summer."

"There's so much to do around here. I'll have to show you all of the best places to hang out." He grinned as he looked over at me. "I can be your tour guide—if you want."

"Oh, that's so nice of you, but I'm sure you have plenty of better things to do."

"That's the best part of this summer job. Once you put your hours in, you're free the rest of the time." He shrugged. "This is my third year spending the summer here so I've gotten to know quite a bit about the area. My friend Frankie and I stay in a house owned by the club. It's right on the beach. We share it with another lifeguard and a waitress from the club." He pointed down the beach in the direction of a large house. "It's not far. We usually have parties on the weekends."

I smiled and nodded at him. He probably wanted me to know about the parties so that I'd invite Kelsie. I'd been in this position before. But I didn't mind. I was sure that Kelsie would love to go.

"Sounds like you know how to have a great summer." I reached down to pick up a multi-colored shell and held it up to the dimming sunlight. "What a treasure!"

"Good find." He looked at the shell, then shifted his focus to me. "So many people don't even bother to look."

"Here." I pressed the shell into the palm of his hand and winked at him. "It's for you."

"For me?" He raised his eyebrows, then smiled. "Why? You found it, you should keep it."

"It's a thank you." I shrugged. "For what you did for me today."

"It's my job." He slipped the shell into the pocket of his shorts and kept his eyes on me.

"I know." I felt my cheeks flush for about the hundredth time that day. "But I'm still grateful—and embarrassed." A light breeze from the water tugged a few loose strands of my hair into my face as I glanced away from him.

"Hey, don't be." His fingertips brushed my hair away and he met my eyes again. "The ocean—it's stronger than anyone knows. It can catch even the most experienced by surprise."

"Thanks." I took a slight step back as my heart raced. Unable to look at him, I turned my attention to the sky. "Wow." I whispered the word as a myriad of colors sprawled above us.

"Yeah." He released a slow breath as he looked up as well.

"It's getting late." I felt a little awkward as I turned back toward the beach club.

"Jaxx." He caught my hand for just a second, before his own fell back to his side. "Hey, maybe next time, you'll be able to get in on our volleyball game. We play nearly every evening after work."

"Yeah, I really want to try that. Okay, well, I better get going. I guess I'll probably see you tomorrow—at the beach club."

"See you then!" He waved to me, then jogged off down the beach.

SEVEN

I gathered my hair—still damp from the shower—into a tight ponytail, then let it drape down my back. The house was so quiet, I could hear the waves on the beach, even though they were two blocks away.

Mr. Celeste had left early that morning for another business meeting. I'd heard the door close behind him before daylight. Hannah and the kids were sound asleep, and I had an hour before I was officially on duty.

I'd always been an early riser, thanks to spending a lot of time on my grandfather's farm. I couldn't seem to break the habit—even at the beach. I had some pent-up energy from missing out on the volleyball game the night before and I knew that a good run would release it.

I slipped out of the house as quietly as I could, then cut across the street in the direction of the beach club. The day before, the beach had been packed, but since the club wasn't open yet, there were no cars parked in the lot.

As I stepped onto the sand, I was greeted by an empty beach.

The sight of the ocean thrilled me, just as it had the day

before, but now I looked at it with a deeper sense of respect. I broke into a run and let the salty air fill my lungs.

As my feet dug into the sand, my muscles flexed and I felt my heart begin to pound. The adrenaline of a good workout was one of the reasons why I loved sports so much. I never felt freer than when I pushed myself as far as I could and then just an inch further.

As I passed by the large homes that lined the beach, I imagined what it might be like to live in one—to grow up spending the summers in one. Hannah had mentioned spending her teenage years at the beach. Had she run across the same sand? The thought brought a smile to my lips.

The sight of Nate on the deck of one of the houses made my smile spread wider. Without breaking my stride, I waved to him.

"Jaxx!" He waved back, then launched himself right off the side of the deck and onto the sand not far from me.

I admired the fluid way his body moved and guessed that he had to be an athlete of some kind himself.

"Can I join you?"

Thrilled to have a running partner—mainly because it meant that I had competition—I looked straight into his eyes and grinned.

"That depends, can you keep up?" I burst into a sprint.

I heard his laughter right behind me and felt a light spray of sand against my ankles as he chased after me.

The ocean breeze flowed across my skin as I ran even faster. It didn't take much to spark my competitive nature and I loved having a worthy rival.

Within a few minutes he'd caught up with me and I could tell from his long strides that he was trying to overtake me.

"No you don't!" I flashed him a grin as I used my reserve energy to burst into another sprint.

"Jaxx!" He gasped out my name as he laughed and did his best to keep up.

I glanced back at him and saw his foot slide forward through the sand. I knew that he was about to fall even before he did. By the time he landed in the sand, I'd jogged back toward him.

"You okay?" I held my hand out to help him up.

"Fine, just a little embarrassed." He smiled as he grabbed my hand and let me help him up.

"Why? Because I beat you?" I stared into his eyes.

"No. I'm totally impressed about that. Most girls around here spend all their time lying on the beach. It's great to have someone around that can show me up." He winked at me. "I'm embarrassed because I slipped." He hesitated, as if he might have more to say, then cleared his throat. "I guess I got distracted."

"By the sunrise?" I smiled.

"Yeah, that must have been it." He stared into my eyes, then nodded. "Oh, and by the way, I'm going to want a rematch."

"Any time!" I kicked a bit of sand playfully in his direction. "I mean—after you recover a bit."

"Ouch!" He shook his head. "Are you this rough on all the guys?"

"Nope, just the ones that can almost beat me." I crossed my arms. "Almost."

"Almost." He repeated. "Well, we still have to run back, you know!"

"I'll give you a head start."

"Sweet!" He didn't waste a second of it as he sprinted off.

I chased after him, but soon we were both winded and we gave in to a light jog.

"I'm going to surf after this. You should come with me." He glanced over at me. "Unless you're afraid of getting back in the water?"

"Not at all! I can't wait to get back in. But I have to be at work by seven." I frowned. "I'd love to learn how to surf, though." I looked out over the water. "I can only imagine what it must feel like to be on top of one of those waves."

"Let me teach you." He slowed to a walk beside me. "I know you'll love it."

"Really? That would be awesome! I'm off tomorrow."

"Me too. Perfect. We can figure it out later at the beach club." He slowed down even more as we neared his house. "Do you have any other plans for your day off?"

"Not sure yet. Kelsie and I are dying to check out New York City, but I'm not sure we're ready for that yet." I shrugged.

"Oh, I know some great spots in the city. It's where I grew up." He lifted his shoulders in a slight shrug. "It was always just me and my dad, so we did a lot of dining out."

"Great, I'll have to pick your brain about the best places to go." I watched as he waved and headed off toward his house.

Maybe yesterday had started off rough but getting to know Nate had turned out to be a great thing. Now I had a partner in crime, someone that I could be myself around, someone who wasn't afraid to challenge me.

I jogged back toward the house, buzzing with excitement at the idea of learning how to surf.

EIGHT

I dug the moat around the castle a little deeper as Bella walked up to me with her bucket half full of water. With each step she spilled a little bit more.

"Good job." I took the bucket from her as she plopped down in the sand beside me.

"We need fishies!" She clapped her hands and grinned.

"Hm, I hadn't thought of that." I positioned the bucket of water near the edge of the moat, then helped her tip the contents into the moat. "Maybe we should get sharks instead?"

"Shark!" Anthony screamed as loud as he could.

"What? Where?!" Kelsie jumped up from the towel she had just sprawled out on and snatched Cherish up out of the sand and into her arms.

A few other people nearby looked in our direction, then warily out at the sea.

"There's no shark!" I held up my hand and laughed. "Just a little boy's imagination." I looked toward the lifeguard stand in time to catch Nate laughing. I rolled my eyes and laughed as well.

"Okay, good." Kelsie set Cherish back down in the sand. "Oh, that gives me an idea. We should make a sand sculpture!"

"A what?" Cherish stared at her.

"We could make a shark—out of sand." She sat down beside the little girl. "Want to try?"

"Sure." Cherish smiled and grabbed a shovel.

As I did my best to maintain peace between Bella and Anthony, I noticed a few people gathered around the lifeguard stand. I recognized one of the guys as Nate's friend, Frankie—the co-worker that had relieved his shift from the day before. Beside him was another guy, a bit taller than Frankie, and quite muscular. Two girls also lingered close to the lifeguard stand, the taller of the two with her foot propped up on one of the steps. Her long brown hair caught every ray of sunlight that it could as it wafted around her shoulders. The girl beside her had bright red hair that Frankie seemed to be fascinated with.

"Hello up there!" The taller girl waved at Nate.

Nate waved back but kept his eyes on the water.

I turned back to Anthony just in time to see him smash through the moat that Bella and I had built.

"Anthony, no!" Bella wailed.

"Shark!" Anthony giggled as he put one hand on the other in an attempt to look like a shark.

Sensing the impending meltdown, I knew I had to do something.

"I'm a shark hunter!" I jumped to my feet.

"No!" Anthony gasped and giggled at the same time. Then he started to run.

As I chased after him, Nate scooped him up into his arms.

"Trust me, buddy, that's one race you're not going to win." He laughed as he handed Anthony over to me and we walked back toward our spot on the beach.

"Thanks for catching my shark." I wiggled my eyebrows. "Now he has to spend some time in shark jail."

"Jaxx! There's no such thing as shark jail!" Cherish put her hands on her hips as she stared at me.

"Yes, there is! That's why they're always in cages." Bella huffed. "You're going to shark jail, Anthony!"

"No!" Anthony wailed.

"Don't worry, guys." Nate crouched down in front of all three of them. "There are no shark jails at the beach. Besides, I don't think Anthony is a shark at all." He peered at Anthony. "Aren't you really a dolphin?"

"Yup!" Anthony grinned.

"Oh, okay. Dolphins can be in my moat." Bella sat back as Anthony stomped through the moat around her castle.

"Wow, you just saved me again." I laughed as I met Nate's eyes.

"I don't mind. Kids are great." He shrugged.

"Nate!" The blonde girl walked toward him. "I've been waiting to talk to you all day! How did you slip past me?"

"Oh, it's Frankie's turn to keep watch." Nate smiled at her. "Maby, it's good to see you."

"You too." She stared straight into his eyes. "So glad summer is finally here."

"This is Jaxx." He gestured to me, then to Kelsie. "And Kelsie. They're new here this summer."

"Oh, how nice." Maby offered a slight smile to each of us. "Listen, since you're off work, maybe we could grab a soda?" She ran her fingertips lightly across his shoulder. "I'm sure you could use a break from the sun."

"Sure, I'm pretty thirsty." He glanced at me. "Oh, Jaxx, you should put my number in your phone so we can set a time for our surfing lesson."

"Sure." I grabbed my phone out of my beach bag and typed in the numbers he rattled off.

"Nate?" Maby grabbed his hand and gave it a light tug. "I'm not going to wait forever, you know."

"Sorry." He grinned at her. "See you all later." He waved to us, then walked with Maby's arm wrapped around his.

"Surfing?" Kelsie scooted across the sand toward me.

"Oh yeah, I ran into him on my run this morning and he offered to teach me." I rubbed my palms together. "I can't wait to get on top of one of those waves!"

"Hm, I'm sure that's not what he's planning to get on— "

"Kelsie!" I gave her a firm shove. "Don't talk like that in front of the kids."

"Sorry, sorry." Kelsie rolled her eyes. "Anyway, I'm glad you have a date. That means that I have my morning free to continue my hunt."

"It's not a date!" I groaned. "He's just a really nice guy. I'm glad I've gotten the chance to get to know him a little bit and I can't wait to learn everything I can about surfing from him. You don't mind, do you? I know it's our first day off."

"No, I don't mind at all. I'm sure I can occupy myself. We can get together later in the afternoon." She tilted her head to the side as she looked toward the beach club where Nate and Maby had disappeared. "I wonder if those two are a thing. She was hanging all over him."

"Maybe." I shrugged. "She seems like his type."

"You know his type?" She laughed.

"Honestly, it's just a guess. I'm not the least bit interested in who his type is." I grinned. "Now tell me more about this hunt. Any potential prey I should know about? Maybe Frankie?"

"Nah, Frankie isn't who I'm looking for. But his friend? The big guy? Yeah, I might just have to hunt him down."

"Good luck!" I winked at her.

NINE

After a busy evening with the kids, I was ready for a good night's sleep. But the moment I closed my eyes, my thoughts filled with images of the ocean. Even lying still in my bed, I thought about the way the waves had spun me—the way the current had tugged at me. My heartbeat quickened, but not because of fear.

Instead, I was excited. I looked forward to going back out into the water, this time with an ally who would be able to help me navigate all the new challenges of the ocean. I imagined hopping right up on the board and sailing along just fine on a giant wave.

Perhaps my expectations were a little high.

I'd received a text from Nate earlier that evening asking if sunrise was too early to meet. I thought it would be perfect. But as I continued to have trouble falling asleep, I hoped that I wouldn't end up too exhausted.

The next thing I knew, my alarm was ringing.

Groggily, I swiped off the alarm, then stared at the time on my phone. For a moment I thought about going back to sleep. It was my day off, after all. I had nowhere to be.

Then I remembered.

"Surfing!" I jumped out of bed, then winced as I wondered if I'd been too noisy.

The quiet house indicated that I hadn't woken anyone.

I pulled on my bathing suit, tied my hair back, and headed straight out the door.

As excited as I was, I felt a pang of dread too. Nate had already seen me embarrass myself in the ocean. What if I made a fool of myself as I tried to learn to surf?

I'd always been willing to try my hand at any new sport that crossed my path, but the initial learning process made me a little on edge. I had a strong drive to accomplish whatever I set out to do, and if I failed, it could hit me pretty hard. My little sister Lucy called it my biggest flaw. She claimed I was a perfectionist.

But to me it wasn't about perfection. It was about skill and the thrill of mastery. I wanted to win, even when I was the only person I was competing against. It wasn't about being the best, it was about knowing that I could do it.

As I walked across the sandy beach, I prepared myself for the idea that it might be quite a struggle. But the sight of Nate at the edge of the water with two surfboards beside him erased that anxiety. He hadn't given me a hard time about having to rescue me the day before. I doubted he would give me a hard time if I fell off the board a few times.

He looked over his shoulder and smiled at me. Framed by the sunrise, his lean body glistened with droplets of sea water. His slicked-back hair indicated he'd already gone for a dip. As his green eyes met mine, they were full of warmth and excitement and for just a second, I couldn't breathe.

The moment felt perfect, beyond anything I'd ever experienced before.

If every day of my summer in the Hamptons would be filled

with moments like this, I doubted that I would ever want to go back home. How lucky was I to have made such a good friend?

"Are you ready for this?" He grinned as he handed me one of the boards.

"I'm always ready." I smirked as I took the board from him.

All of the insecurity I'd felt on my way to the water vanished the moment I felt the smooth board in my grasp. It didn't matter how many times I might fall off. I knew that I would figure it out, especially with Nate's help.

As he walked me through the process of paddling on the board, I found it easy to accomplish.

"I've done some paddle boarding on a lake back home, so I'm guessing this is pretty similar."

"It is, with one big difference." He balanced himself on his board, then looked back at me. "Waves."

I pulled myself up the way he showed me and found my balance almost instantly. "Like this?" I held my arms out to stabilize myself.

"Impressive!" He stared at me for a long moment. "You must have a very strong core."

"I am pretty active and—" Before I could finish my statement, the board slipped right out from under me and I crashed down into the water.

"Jaxx!" He jumped off his board beside me.

I laughed as I popped back up out of the water and clung to my board. "Okay, maybe I need a little more practice."

"You did great." His eyes locked to mine, then he sprawled out across his board. "Let's go find you your first wave."

My heart pounded at the thought. For the first time ever, I was really going to surf.

As I paddled out after him, I realized that I trusted his expertise. I didn't question for a second that he would make sure I was safe. It was refreshing to have such a good teacher.

"Okay, the key here is rhythm." He looked over at me. "It's not just about seeing the wave, it's about feeling it. Every wave is a little different. If you go too early or too late, you're not going to have a good ride." He gestured for me to come closer to his side. "Close your eyes."

"What? But I won't be able to see the wave." I frowned.

"Like I said, it's about feeling." He took my hand off the board and placed it in the water. As he pulled his hand away, I felt the water flowing around my fingers. "Learning the language of the ocean uses all of your senses. Hearing will tell you the strength of the wave. Smell will warn you if the weather's about to change. Seeing will alert you to that perfect swell, but feeling will tell you when the moment is just right."

TEN

As I closed my eyes, I began to experience what Nate had described. Even without seeing the wave, I could sense its rise— and its strength. When I opened my eyes, I saw him crouched on his board.

"Here's a good one. Just try to follow what I do. Remember..." He glanced back at me. "If you don't get it the first time, don't be too hard on yourself."

I raised an eyebrow as I realized how well he knew me already. Then I got into position as well.

As the wave began to rise, I watched Nate rise with it. His strong frame curved and flowed as fluidly as the wave that he sailed across.

I did my best to mimic his every move and I soon found myself above the water on the curve of the wave.

"Yes!" Nate shouted at me. "You did it, Jaxx! You're doing it!"

As thrilling as it was to sail with the wave, the pride in his voice and genuine excitement in his expression seemed to lift me even higher.

After a few more waves, we headed back to the shore.

"I can't believe how fast you picked that up." He shook some water from his hair, then smiled at me. "You're a natural."

"You're a great teacher." I brushed my ponytail back over my shoulder. "I hope we can do it again sometime. Maybe next time, we can try some bigger ones?" I raised an eyebrow. "I know you were taking it easy on me."

"You don't miss a thing, do you?" He grinned. "I'd love to do it again. Are you busy tonight?"

"Oh, night surfing could be fun." I glanced back over the water.

"No, not night surfing." He laughed. "At least not this time. A group of us are going out to Frankie's dad's cafe. It's a little place on the beach—great live music and a fantastic view. You should come." He met my eyes.

"Maybe." I shrugged. "I'll have to see what Kelsie is doing."

"You should bring her. You'll both have a great time." He smiled as he stepped a little closer to me. "Remember, I'm your tour guide." He plucked a bit of seaweed from my hair and tossed it to the sand.

"Well, you were right about surfing, so I'm sure you're right about this place too." I felt a rush of excitement at the thought of live music. "What's the name of the place? Maybe we'll meet up with all of you later."

"Breakers Cafe." He picked up both surfboards. "Hope to see you there."

As he walked away, I turned back to face the ocean. Surfing had been an amazing experience and I couldn't wait to learn more about it. I messaged Kelsie with the invite and our meeting time, then I walked back to the house to shower and change.

The moment I arrived at her door, she began to chatter.

"So, how was surfing? Did he push you off the board so he could rescue you again?" She cooed as she walked beside me toward the shops.

"What?" I laughed. "No of course not. He's a great teacher. Kelsie, it was such an amazing feeling."

"Being with him?" She pursed her lips in a playful kissing motion.

"Stop it!" I rolled my eyes. "No, being on the wave. It was incredible. You really have to try it."

"Not my thing." She scrunched up her nose. "But tonight will be. I can't wait to dance. Which is why we have to go shopping. We both need something to wear."

"I'm planning on wearing this." I gestured to my fitted t-shirt and jean shorts.

"No." Kelsie cleared her throat. "Absolutely not. I won't stand for that."

"Kelsie, it's a cafe, not a fashion show."

"See, that's where you're wrong. It's a gathering, with all the best people in the Hamptons, all of the people we want to spend our time with all summer long. It's important to make a good impression. Besides, what if Maby is there? I'm sure she'll be dressed in something stunning." She pulled me into one of the shops.

"Why would I care what Maby is wearing?" I stared at her. "Did you get too much sun or something?"

"Jaxx. She's obviously got a thing for Nate. You have to stake your claim before she gets those manicured nails dug in too deep." She glanced at my hands. "Speaking of nails, we should stop by the salon and see if they can do anything with yours."

"Kelsie, enough!" I sighed. "Look, I know you're all about romance, but that's not what's happening with me and Nate. We're just friends—I think we're getting to be good friends, actually. I'm sure he and Maby will be perfectly happy together. As long as he still surfs with me, I really don't care who he dates."

"If you say so." She eyed me for a moment. "But a new dress couldn't hurt, right?"

"Honestly, I'm pretty worn out from surfing this morning. I'm only going because you want to go." I pointed out a dress hanging on the wall. "That looks like your style—off the shoulder and bright."

"You are so right!" She snatched it up. "Yes, you have to go tonight." She looked straight at me. "You can't leave me all alone. Besides, you're the one that Nate invited."

"He invited both of us. Everyone from the beach club is going." I shrugged and glanced through a collection of sports-themed shirts. My eyes lingered on one that featured the silhouette of a surfer against a bright sun. "Maybe I will get something." I picked up the t-shirt as she disappeared into the dressing room.

"Oh, this is great!" Kelsie stepped out of the dressing room and did a quick twirl that caused the skirt of her dress to spin. "I like it." She met my eyes. "But it would look so much better on you."

"Yeah, right." I crossed my arms as she placed her hands on her hips. "Give it up, Kelsie. I'm going tonight—that's the most you're getting out of me."

"Maybe we could take your hair down?" She pouted as she tugged at my ponytail.

"No thanks." I brushed her hand away and laughed.

"Well, I am going to find someone to share some summer dates with. So, you'd better figure out who you can tolerate, because there are going to be some double dates. If not Nate, then what about his friend Frankie?"

"No way!" I shook my head as she launched into another spiel about a makeover. I tuned her out and paid for my t-shirt.

ELEVEN

"Are you ready yet?" I leaned my head against the bathroom door and sighed.

"Beauty takes time, Jaxx!" Kelsie called out from behind the door.

"Hours? Does it take hours?" I moaned.

"It's only been twenty minutes!" she shouted back.

"Twenty minutes." I crossed my arms. "Maybe if you don't count the first hour or the one after that." I rolled my eyes.

Ever since we'd arrived back at Kelsie's place so that she could get ready to go out, I'd been waiting. I'd played with Cherish a bit, but then she and her parents had gone out for the night.

I glanced at my phone and noticed a text from Nate. Attached was a picture of the outdoor patio of the cafe. There was a band, people dancing, and in the distance, I could see the beach.

"Okay, that does look like fun." I smiled as I texted him back. "Let's go, Kelsie!" I pounded on the door. "I want to get there before the band leaves for the night."

"Alright, alright." Kelsie stepped out of the bathroom and

fluffed her perfectly groomed hair. "How do I look?" She spun around in her new dress.

"Gorgeous, just like you did two hours ago!" I grabbed her hand and pulled her toward the door. "Now let's go before I change my mind. I do have a good book I could be reading, you know."

"You'd take a book over time with Nate?" She followed me out the door and into the street.

"Well, I guess that depends on what we're doing. If we're surfing, Nate wins. But if we're doing something boring, a good book would definitely be better."

"Sure." She winked at me.

"Huh?" I stared at her. Then I shook my head. "You know what? Never mind. Let's see if you can keep up!" I broke into a run.

"No fair! I'm wearing heels!" she shouted as she hobbled after me.

After a few minutes I slowed down so that she could catch up. "Oh, there you are." I grinned.

"So funny. Do you think I spend that long on my make-up just to sweat it off?" She made a face.

"I'm not sure why you spend so much time on your make-up." I looked over at her. "You're already so beautiful. You look great with the make-up too, but why bother when you're already so pretty?"

"Just because you think I'm pretty, doesn't mean I am." She shrugged. "Besides, it's expected. Guys like it when you put some effort into the way you look. It makes them feel special—like you want to look your best for them."

"Really?" I scrunched up my nose at the thought. "If I had to do that to make a guy feel special, I think I'd lose my mind."

"You'll see one day." She smiled at me. "You're lucky, you know."

"I am? How?" I paused in front of the cafe and turned to face her.

"You never worry about the way you look. You never care about impressing people. You're always happy with whatever you're wearing—you never go out of your way to get anyone's attention. I wish I could be like that sometimes."

"No, you don't." I grinned as I looked into her eyes.

"Okay, fine, I don't!" She grabbed my hand. "Let's go dance!"

"Oh, I don't know about that!" I pulled back as she dragged me through the cafe and out onto the crowded patio.

"I do!" She continued to tug me until I was in the middle of the dance floor with a group of other people, all moving and swaying to the lively song that the band was playing. "Now dance with me!"

I sighed, glanced around for an escape, then gave in. As I tried to keep up with her movement, I heard a voice not far from me.

"Nice shirt!"

I turned and looked right into Nate's eyes. "Thanks." I smiled. "I just got it."

"You certainly earned it. I've never seen anyone take to the waves like you did." He stepped closer to me and soon he, Kelsie, and I were all dancing together.

"I love this band." I glanced at the group on a slightly elevated stage. "Do you know them?"

"They're just a local band, but they play here every summer." He tipped his head toward the drummer. "He and Frankie grew up together."

"Nice." I smiled as I looked back at him. "I see you're the person to know around here."

"Some people think so." He grinned as he looked into my eyes. "I'm glad you came out tonight."

"Well, Kelsie was into it. I was a little worn out after surfing, to be honest." I ran my hand along my stomach. "Quite an ab work-out."

"Isn't it?" He laughed as he patted his own stomach.

"Oh, there you are, Nate!" Maby pushed past me and stopped right between Nate and me. "I thought you were getting me a drink?"

"Oh right, sorry. I saw Jaxx and Kelsie and just wanted to say hi." He shrugged. "Did you two want a drink? I can grab us all something."

"Oh, forget it, I'll just get it myself." Maby rolled her eyes, then stalked off through the crowd.

"Is she okay?" I raised my eyebrows.

"Just thirsty, I'm sure." Kelsie smirked as she watched Maby walk away.

"I'd better get those drinks." Nate walked off after Maby.

"That girl is really pushing my buttons." Kelsie narrowed her eyes as she walked off of the dance floor. "You need to set her straight."

"Set her straight about what?" I frowned as I followed her.

"Kelsie!" Frankie's and Nate's friend waved to her from the other side of the patio.

"Oh, there's Lance, I'll be back!" She hurried over to him.

I sighed as I walked over to an empty table, doubting she'd be back anytime soon. Once Kelsie had her eyes on the prize, she often forgot about everything else. I had been looking forward to a fun night, but as I looked over the crowd of faces I didn't know, I realized that I still didn't quite fit in.

TWELVE

I woke up the next morning, eager to enjoy another day off. Kelsie and I planned to check out some sights and spend some time at the beach. My phone rang just as I was ready to walk out the door to meet her.

"Kelsie, I'm on my way."

"Don't bother." She sighed. "Patti had an emergency with a friend and she needs me to stay with Cherish so she can go help her."

"Oh, that sounds bad." I frowned. "Is everything okay?"

"Not sure yet. I get the feeling it's more about emotional support than anything else. Hey listen, I'm sorry about ditching you last night."

"Don't worry about it. Did you have fun with Lance?" I smiled.

"We had a nice walk on the beach. I like him, but he's a little...I don't know." She paused.

"Boring?"

"Very." She huffed. "Why can't they ever be cute and interesting?"

"Maybe when you get to know him better, he'll turn out to

be more interesting." I walked back into my room and sat down on the edge of my bed.

"I hope so. I guess I'll have to find out. Nate seems like a lot of fun though."

"He is. He doesn't even mind when I beat him at something." I smiled at the memory of him hitting the sand during our race on the beach.

"That's a great quality—I guess?" She laughed. "Well, I'd better go be a pony for Cherish."

"Have fun!" I neighed like a horse, laughed, and then hung up the phone.

I looked at the book on my bedside table that I'd been meaning to read. I picked it up and began to thumb through it. Usually, I enjoyed slipping into a different world for a little while. But now, the words didn't leap off the page. Instead, I felt like I was wasting my time. I wanted to live my story, not read about someone else's.

The summer would only last so long. Did I want to spend it holed up in my room?

I felt the urge to call Kelsie again, but I knew she was busy with Cherish. If only I knew a few more people maybe I'd have someone to do something with. I thought about exploring the beach town, but without knowing where I was going, I figured it could get frustrating.

Finally, I decided to call Nate. Maybe he would want to run with me or even fit in a surfing lesson. I had to do something with my time.

As the phone rang, I winced and hoped that I wouldn't be interrupting something between him and Maby. Kelsie seemed pretty convinced that they were a couple. I found it hard to believe that he'd be into her after the way she'd acted at the cafe, but guys could be very strange that way.

I was about to hang up when he answered the phone.

"Jaxx, I was just thinking about you."

"You were?" I smiled. "Were you thinking about wanting a rematch on the beach? Maybe you'll be able to keep up with me this time?"

"Oh, I definitely want a rematch." He laughed. "But no, that's not what I was thinking. Actually, I was hoping you might be free this afternoon. Do you already have plans?"

"Not at all. That's why I called. I'm bored and Kelsie is working. I need something to do. I thought maybe we could run or surf if you're free."

"I'd like to do either of those things, but unfortunately I already have plans."

"Oh, that's okay." I guessed that his plan might have to do with Maby.

"I'm going to this volleyball match. It's semi-professional and a local team is competing. They're really good. I have an extra ticket and I wondered if you liked watching volleyball?"

"Absolutely!" I jumped up off of the edge of my bed and smiled. "I'll be happy to take that ticket off your hands."

"So, I can pick you up in about twenty minutes? Or do you need some time to get ready?"

I glanced down at my plain top and shorts. "No, I'm good to go. Thanks so much. This will be fun." I caught myself before I could add, "especially with you". He might take that the wrong way. But it really did make it so much better that he would be by my side as we watched. Instinctively, I felt that it was something that we'd both enjoy.

"Great, I'll be there soon."

I hung up the phone, then I grabbed some water and a snack from the kitchen and headed out to the front porch to wait for him.

He pulled up in a green jeep.

"Wow!" I climbed in beside him. "Is this yours?"

"All mine." He grinned. "It's nice, huh?"

"Very! I've always wanted a jeep."

"Well, then you're going to enjoy the ride." He gunned the engine as he pulled away from the house.

After the short trip to the location of the meet, his phone rang. He glanced at the name on the screen, then put it down again.

"Ready?"

"It's okay if you need to take that."

"No way, I don't want to miss a second. Let's go." He led the way to the bleachers.

As I settled in beside him, I could sense that he was as excited as I was. The bleachers filled up fast and we were pushed close together by the people beside us.

About halfway through the game, he slipped away and returned with a tray filled with snacks and two drinks.

"You do eat, right?" He sat down beside me.

"What?" I grabbed a cheese fry before he could answer.

"Sorry, it's just—sometimes girls are picky about what they eat."

"I guess you've been hanging out with the wrong girls then." I grabbed one of the sodas from the tray. "Thanks for this, but you'd better eat fast, because those cheese fries are really good."

"Thanks for the warning." He grabbed a few as I went back for more.

Our hands collided for a brief second and suddenly I felt awkward.

He gave my hand a light smack and took the fry I'd been reaching for. "Don't take all the cheesy ones!"

"I told you, you have to be quick around me." I laughed as I snatched another fry. "I should give you some cash for this."

"Don't worry about that." He shifted closer on the bleacher

beside me. "I know you mentioned wanting to see the city. Want to join me next Sunday?"

"That would be fantastic. I can't believe we have the same days off."

"Me either. It works out perfectly." He pointed to the court. "Oh, watch this, it's going to be amazing!"

"What?" I stared at the players as they waited for the match to start again.

"Who's fast now?" He snagged a fry full of cheese while I wasn't looking.

"Oh, now it's on!" I laughed as we continued to fight over the fries.

THIRTEEN

Even though the day hadn't gone as I'd originally planned, it ended up being wonderful. I spent my evening thinking about the places I'd like to visit in New York City and wondering if Nate would be able to show them all to me.

By the time I felt myself drifting off to sleep, every cell in my body buzzed with excitement for next Sunday. I just had to get through the week and then I would be in the big city. I couldn't imagine a better tour guide than Nate. He seemed to know everything, and he carried himself with such confidence—without being arrogant about it.

I woke up the next day, feeling eager to hit the beach.

The light patter of rain against my window signaled that things were going to unfold quite differently.

"Sorry, kids, no beach today." Hannah sighed as she placed pancakes on each of their plates. "It's never any fun when it rains here in the summer."

"Is it going to keep going all day?" I peered out through the kitchen window.

"Yes, in fact, unless something changes, it's supposed to rain all week." She winced as she looked at me. "I'm sorry, it's going to be a tough one with these two wild creatures."

"But I want to go to the beach!" Bella moaned and flopped her hands against the table. "Please! Why can't we?"

"It's raining, sweetie." Hannah shook her head.

"Rain is wet. The ocean is wet! So what?" Bella huffed.

"It's not safe to be on the beach if it's stormy, Bella." I sat down beside her. "Listen, we'll have lots of fun inside today." I glanced over at Hannah. "Would it be okay if I invite Kelsie and Cherish over?"

"That's a perfect idea. Patti and I have to go to the same lunch meeting today." She looked straight at Bella. "You're going to be a good girl for Jaxx, right?"

"Yes!" Bella squealed. "I get to play with Cherish!"

"First you have to eat your breakfast." I pointed to her plate.

I smiled for Cherish, but I couldn't hide my own disappointment. A rainy week meant no runs or surfing lessons. I didn't do well when I didn't have a lot of physical activity.

When Kelsie and Cherish arrived, the three kids began to destroy the playroom. They dumped buckets of well-organized toys everywhere.

"What a mess!" Kelsie frowned. "Maybe we should clean up?"

"Don't bother." I waved my hand. "I'll put it all back together when they're done. Trust me, if we clean up now, they'll just dump them all back out again."

"Kids." Kelsie flopped down in a chair and looked over at me. "So, what's this I hear about you going to a volleyball game with Nate yesterday?"

"How did you hear about that?" I raised my eyebrows.

"Oh, there's been some chatter. From what I hear, he was supposed to go with Maby, but she bailed at the last minute."

"He didn't tell me that." I frowned. "I guess that doesn't make her like me any more than she already does."

"What I want to know is why you didn't tell me?" Kelsie frowned. "We're supposed to be best friends, remember?"

"I was going to tell you. But I knew that you'd start teasing me about it being a date and it wasn't." I sighed.

"Hm, he invited you to an event? He paid for the ticket? Wait, did he buy you any food?" She sat forward in her chair.

"Just some snacks." I shrugged.

"Your own snacks or shared snacks?" She looked straight into my eyes.

"Shared." I smiled as I thought about our fight over the fries. "He was impressed by my appetite, I think."

"Okay." She tilted her head to the side. "That's a little odd. But it's definitely a date."

"See! This is why I didn't tell you." I rolled my eyes. "Kelsie, Nate is my friend. He's a great friend. So good in fact that he offered to take us to New York City next Sunday. He'll show us around, so we won't have to stumble about like tourists."

"That sounds great." She ducked as a ball flew past her head. "But did he actually invite both of us?"

"Of course he did." I reviewed what he'd said in my mind. Maybe he hadn't mentioned Kelsie, but I was sure he meant to invite her too.

"Okay, if you say so." She stood up from the chair, retrieved the ball, and tossed it back to the kids. "You were right about Lance, by the way. I talked to him for a while on the phone last night and he is actually pretty interesting. I was ready to write him off, but thanks to you, now I know he has a secret love for art and fashion."

"Fashion?" I laughed.

"He promised to show me his closet." She grinned.

"Okay, it sounds like you two definitely have some things in common."

"Yeah. We like similar things. Kind of like you and Nate both like sports." She ducked again and this time the ball sailed past and hit me square in the forehead.

"Hey! Be careful, please!" I rubbed my head as I tossed the ball back to them. "Kelsie, drop it, please. It's just annoying."

"Alright, I'll be good, I promise." She sat down on the arm of my chair. "It's just that I worry about you. You haven't really dated anyone since swimmer boy. I don't want you to end up alone."

"You don't have to worry about me, I'll be fine. I don't need to date a lot to find the right one. I'm sure when I meet him, I'll know it." I looked up at her. "I'd rather go straight for the goal than waste my time on awkward dates."

"How will you know?" She met my eyes. "I've met so many guys that excited me so much at first and then it just fizzled out. How are you going to know when you've found the right one?"

"I don't know. Little birds singing in the air, random stars shining in the sky?" I grinned.

"I'm serious, Jaxx." She shook her head. "I used to think that I'd meet my prince in some great romantic way. But now..." She shrugged. "I don't know, I guess I'm just not so sure about it."

"You're losing faith in romance?" I frowned as I studied her. "Why? What's wrong?"

"It's just not quite the summer I was hoping for." She smiled, then walked off to play with the kids.

FOURTEEN

By the fourth rainy day, we were all a little stir crazy. I jumped at the opportunity to take the kids to the beach club for lunch.

"At least it will get them out for a bit. It's just drizzling today, so it shouldn't be too bad." Hannah handed out raincoats to the kids. "I wouldn't mind if you let them jump in a few puddles."

"Great." I smiled as I pulled on my own jacket. "I'll make sure they do."

"Can't we go swimming yet?" Bella sighed. "It's just a little rain."

"Not quite yet, it's a bit too chilly." I patted the top of her head as I recalled how cold the water had been on a sunny day. I didn't want to imagine what it might be like on a cloudy day.

If Nate had texted me with an offer to surf, though, I would have done anything to make it happen. He hadn't. At least not about surfing. He'd sent me a few funny pictures of volleyball fails and a list of places we might like to visit in New York City, but that had tapered off as the rain had continued.

Luckily, the weather report indicated a break in the gloom over the next few days.

Until then, a meal at the club would have to be enough of an outing to please the kids.

As we walked in the direction of the club, I pointed out the biggest puddles for the kids to jump in.

We arrived at the restaurant and found it nearly empty.

"I guess no one is here for lunch today." I picked Anthony up and settled him in a high chair. "We get the place to ourselves." I grinned as I helped Bella into her chair. "What are we going to order?"

"Nuggets!" Anthony squealed.

"Pizza." Bella rubbed her stomach. "Lots of pizza."

I laughed as she leaned back in her chair and sighed.

"I think I'm going to have a cheeseburger and fries." My stomach rumbled at the thought.

I hadn't been able to be very active during the rainy days, though I did manage a short run between rainstorms the day before. I longed for the sun to return so I could have my choice of activities again.

Once I'd placed our order with the waitress, I occupied the kids with coloring pages. As the crayons slid across the paper, I remembered coloring with my sister and the epic fights we'd had over who'd get to use the bright pink crayon first.

"Here you go." The waitress smiled as she placed the plates in front of us. "You're Jaxx, right?"

"Yes." I met her eyes. "I'm sorry, I don't think we've met."

"Not officially. But I've heard a lot about you. Nate's been raving about how fast you took to surfing. I think he's rubbing it in since I still haven't managed to get up on a board." She held her hand out to me. "I'm Sabrina—one of Nate's roommates."

"Oh! It's nice to meet you." I shook her hand, then smiled. "It's a bit tricky at first, but I had some practice paddle-boarding back home."

"Honestly..." She lowered her voice to a whisper and leaned

close. "It's not the surfboard, it's the sharks. Every time I go out that far, I'm too distracted looking for them. Nate tells me all the time that it's nothing to worry about, but how does he know? I've seen enough summer beach movies to know that it's dangerous out there."

"Good point." I laughed.

"You three enjoy." She winked at me, then walked away. I couldn't help but smile at the idea of Nate talking about me surfing. Impressing an athlete like him meant a lot to me.

"Is it ever going to stop raining?" Bella pouted as she looked out through the large window.

"Yes, it will, and when it does, we'll spend the whole day at the beach." I smiled at her.

"Splash, splash!" Anthony giggled, then squirmed in his high chair. "Fries please!" He reached for my plate.

"Good luck with that, little man." Nate called out as he walked up to our table. "She's not very good at sharing."

"That's not true." I grinned as I pushed some fries onto Anthony's plate. "I just like the cheesy ones."

"How are you surviving with all this rain?" He winced. "I've been pulling some shifts at the cafe since the beach hasn't been open for swimming."

"We've been stuck inside and we are over it, right, Bella?" I watched as the tiny girl took a huge bite of her slice of pizza. She chewed and nodded at the same time.

"The good news is that the sun is coming back tomorrow." He smiled at Bella. "You don't have to wait much longer."

"That's great news." I sighed as I plucked one of the fries off my plate.

"It's good timing too. We've got a bonfire party planned for tomorrow night. I thought it might get rained out. But now, it looks like it's on. You'll come, right?"

"Oh—uh—maybe?" I frowned. "I'm not sure what's going on Saturday night yet, but if I'm free, I'll be there."

"Just come out." He shrugged. "It'll be going most of the night. So, once the kids are in bed, you're free, right?"

"Usually." I nodded. The thought of a bonfire on the beach sparked my excitement about the summer again. "It sounds great. I'll make sure Kelsie can come too."

"Great. We can finalize our plans for Sunday." He smiled.

"Oh right, Kelsie and I are both really excited about it." I grabbed the bottle of ketchup before Anthony could squirt it all over his high chair.

"Oh. Okay." He nodded. "That's great. I'll make sure you guys have a good time."

"Thanks again for doing this." I smiled as I met his eyes. "I don't think my summer would be half as great without you around."

"Glad I could be of service." He gave a short bow, then waved to the kids. As he walked toward the door, he glanced back at me. "See you tomorrow night."

"I'll be there." I picked up my phone and sent a text to Kelsie about the party.

FIFTEEN

The next day was filled with sunshine. Kelsie and I hung out on the beach with the kids as we reveled in the return of the warm, clear weather.

"I'm so looking forward to the party." Kelsie laughed as Cherish buried her feet in the sand. "Lance has promised to roast me a few marshmallows."

"How sweet." I grinned. "I'm looking forward to it too. Once I get the kids in bed, I should be able to head over. What about you?"

"It's date night, so I may be a little later. But we'll see. Last week date night didn't go so well."

"Oh, that's too bad. Are they having trouble?"

"I think they're just tired." Kelsie shrugged. "I guess there's an age you get to where a Saturday night at home sounds better than spending the night out."

"I'm not sure I'll ever get there." I laughed. "Being stuck inside the past few days has reminded me of how much I like to be outside."

"Me too."

After a few more hours of sun, we herded the kids off the beach. I waved to Kelsie and then headed down the road toward our house.

Anthony flopped against my shoulder, already exhausted. But Bella skipped in front of me, full of energy. I hoped dinner and a bath would change that.

By the time I tucked them both into bed, it was a little later than I had hoped. My phone buzzed with a text from Kelsie saying that she'd meet me at the party in a few minutes.

Excited, I tossed on some shorts and a sleeveless top. I didn't want to be too hot near the fire and I secretly hoped that there might be enough light left for a volleyball match.

As I walked in the direction of the house, I felt a rush of euphoria. With the sea stretched out beside me, my bare feet in the sand, and my heart racing with the excitement of what might come next, I realized that I had never been happier.

Sure, I'd had moments of victory, but this was different. I felt as if the future was full of opportunity and I knew that, for tonight at least, I'd be spending time with good friends on the beach.

From a distance, I could see the fire already going. A few people were gathered around it, but I was relieved to see that it wasn't a huge crowd.

"Jaxx!" Sabrina waved to me. "So glad you're here. You should rescue Nate. He's overthinking the snacks."

"How do you overthink snacks?" I laughed as I stepped into the house.

The interior was spacious and well-decorated. I found the kitchen and Nate surrounded by several bowls and several bags of chips.

"Nate? You okay in here?" I grinned as he turned to face me.

"Jaxx, do you know how many different kinds of chips there are?"

"Salty and tasty?" I snatched one from one of the bowls.

"Sorry, I know it's crazy. I just want tonight to go well." He emptied another bag of chips into a bowl.

"I thought you threw these parties pretty often?"

"We do, but this is the first one of the summer. It's kind of a kick-off." He grabbed a few of the bowls.

"Let me help you." I grabbed some too and followed him out the door.

As he set them out on the tables, I realized that it might be the first time I'd seen him the least bit flustered. I found it pretty endearing to see such a confident guy nervous about pleasing his friends.

"Jaxx!" Kelsie ran up and flung her arms around me. "Are we about to have a great night or what?"

"Definitely." I hugged her back.

As the sun began to set, most of us gathered around the fire. I noticed that Nate made sure everyone had a drink before he settled onto a wooden bench beside me.

"Now I can relax."

"You're such a good host." I smiled.

"I try." He shrugged.

Someone on the other side of the fire started playing guitar and someone not far from me began to sing along. Kelsie shrieked and laughed as Lance passed her a perfectly roasted marshmallow that almost fell off the skewer.

I soaked in the perfect moment, full of happiness.

Nate leaned close to me. "Thanks for coming tonight."

"Thanks for inviting me. There is absolutely nowhere else I'd rather be right now." I paused, then tilted my head to the side as I smiled at him. "Except maybe night surfing."

"You just love a challenge, don't you?" The flames of the fire were reflected in his green eyes as he stared at me.

"Always." I brushed my ponytail over my shoulder.

"Me too." He rocked back some on the bench, then looked back at the fire.

SIXTEEN

As the guitar player took a break, someone turned on a radio and a few people stood up to dance close to the fire. I watched as Lance wrapped his arms around Kelsie. The two looked like the perfect couple as they swayed, their skin painted by the firelight. I wondered if Kelsie might have a point. Maybe waiting for just the right person did mean missing out on a lot of special moments like this.

"I'll get you another drink." Nate grabbed my empty cup.

"Oh, you don't have to, I can get it." I stood up and took the cup from him. "Did you want something?"

"I'm filled up." He held his cup up.

I headed to the kitchen to replenish my soda. As I walked through the house, I heard two voices near the front door.

"He's here, right?"

"Of course, where else would he be?" Sabrina replied. "You look hot! Is that a new skirt?"

"Yes. Do you think he'll like it?"

"Only one way to find out." Sabrina laughed. "Go out there and get his attention."

I ducked into the kitchen just as Maby walked past me. Her

short skirt was tailored just right to accentuate her long legs and her top accented the rest of her figure perfectly. She really did look amazing.

I glanced down at my jean shorts and wondered for just as second if I could pull off a skirt like that. I knew I could wear it, but would it fall the same? Would I be able to walk in it the way that she did—with that saucy sway? I laughed at the thought, then pushed it from my mind.

With my cup full, I headed back out to the bonfire.

As soon as I spotted Kelsie, she waved me over to a small huddle with her, Lance, Frankie, and Nate.

"Find it okay?" Nate met my eyes.

"Sure, no problem." I smiled. "I saw Maby come in."

"Oh." He glanced over the crowd. "I wasn't sure if she'd come."

"She seemed pretty excited to be here." I shrugged.

"Good." He tipped his head toward the dance floor. "Want to dance? I love this song."

"Uh." I looked at the floor as apprehension mounted within me. Of all the things I could do—which included most every sport—dancing was not something I'd ever managed to do well. "I don't know. I'm not a very good dancer. You're better off with someone else."

"I didn't ask anyone else." He grinned as he looked into my eyes. "With those moves I saw on the surfboard, I'm sure you'll do just fine."

"Go on, Jaxx." Kelsie shoved me with her elbow. "Dance with him." Her eyes sparkled.

"Kelsie!" I glared at her. She'd been at one of our school dances when I'd literally tripped my partner and he ended up having to get a few stitches.

"Let's go, it'll be fun." Nate grabbed me by the hand as if he had no intention of letting go.

My heart pounded. The last thing I wanted was to be embarrassed in front of all my new friends. No one needed to know just how badly I danced.

"Nate, there you are!" Maby called out as she stepped between us, breaking Nate's grasp on my hand. "I've been looking for you." She smoothed down her skirt and smiled sweetly at him. "It's our song—let's dance before it stops playing."

He opened his mouth to speak, but before he could, I jumped in.

"Great! Go for it, you two!" I took a step back and avoided Nate's stare.

Maby grabbed his hand and pulled him toward the dance floor.

As I glanced up at him, his eyes locked to mine and for just a second I thought I noticed a hint of frustration.

"Trust me, Nate, she just saved you a lot of pain and a potential hospital trip." I laughed as Maby swept him out onto the floor.

He smiled, then turned his attention to the girl who wrapped his arms tightly around her waist.

"Jaxx!" Kelsie groaned as she pulled me away from the others. "What are you thinking?"

"What do you mean?" I frowned as she rolled her eyes.

"Don't you see what she's up to?"

"Huh?" I looked toward the dance floor just in time to see Maby rest her head on Nate's shoulder.

"Clearly, she's trying to keep him away from you." Kelsie crossed her arms.

"Away from me?" I shrugged. "Why?"

"Because she's jealous of you." Kelsie stared at me. "Please tell me you're really not this clueless?"

I frowned. "Why would she be jealous of me? I think you're seeing things that aren't there."

"Am I?" She shook her head. "If you say so."

As the party continued, I did notice that every time Nate walked up to me, Maby made sure she was at his side. It didn't bother me, but after what Kelsie had said, it was hard not to focus on it.

As the party wound down, Kelsie and I were some of the last people huddled around the fire.

Nate sat down beside me. I skimmed the area for any sign of Maby as he leaned close to me.

"I feel like we haven't seen much of each other tonight. I wanted to talk to you about our visit to the city tomorrow. We're still on, right?"

"Absolutely!" My heat pounded at the thought. "I can't wait. I want to see everything!"

"I love seeing you so excited about it." He laughed as he shifted closer to me, his knee brushing against mine. "What time do you want to leave?"

"Are you going to the city?" Maby plopped down on the other side of Nate. "I don't remember being invited."

"I figured you'd be busy." He glanced over at her.

"But you didn't ask, so how would you know?" She looked past him at me. "You wouldn't mind if I tagged along, Jaxx, would you? Or maybe you just want Nate all to yourself?"

As her eyes stared into me, I sensed the jealousy in her words. How was it that Kelsie seemed to always be right about these things?

SEVENTEEN

I did my best to force a smile. The thought of spending the day with Maby made New York City seem like not such a fun trip.

"We've already made plans, Maby." Nate shrugged. "But you and I can go another day."

"No, it's fine." I managed a laugh. "The more the merrier, right? I'm sure there are some great places that you can show us too." I sweetened my tone. Maybe if she saw that she had no reason to be jealous of me, we'd still end up having a good day. "We can be ready by seven, right, Kelsie?" I looked over at her as she joined us.

"Seven?" She winced, then reluctantly nodded. "I suppose. I'll have to set a few alarms, though."

"Great. I'll pick you up." Nate stood up and stretched his arms above his head. "I'd better do a last walk around to pick up trash."

"I can help." I started to stand up to join him, but a look from Maby sat me right back down.

"Oh, let me. I always help Nate out after the parties. Don't I?" She plucked an abandoned cup out of the sand.

"Sure, and I appreciate it." He smiled at her. "Besides, you two need to go home and rest up. You have quite an adventure ahead of you tomorrow."

"Sounds good to me." I smiled, then followed Kelsie down the beach in the direction of the beach club.

"Wow, that was tense." Kelsie frowned. "Why didn't you tell her not to come tomorrow?"

"Because I want her to see that she has nothing to worry about with me." I shrugged. "Once she realizes that Nate and I are just friends, she won't have a reason to feel jealous."

"Are you sure about that?" She paused as we reached the street and turned to look at me. "About her not having anything to worry about?"

"Of course I'm sure." I crossed my arms. "Nate is a great guy —a great friend. That's it, no matter how you want to imagine it."

"Jaxx." Kelsie sighed. "I know I'm always giving you a hard time, but I'm serious about this. You should really think about it, and be sure, because if you keep pushing him away, you're going to push him right into her arms."

"Kelsie." I put my hands on her shoulders and stared into her eyes. "Sweetheart, you really need some rest. I'll see you in the morning." I laughed as I walked away.

By the next morning I was so excited to explore New York City that I hadn't even thought about Maby tagging along until I received a text from Nate.

"Nate's on his way. He's already got Maby with him." I looked up at Kelsie, who was leaning against the porch railing.

"How cozy." She rolled her eyes.

"It's going to be fine." I gave her a playful shove. "Lighten up. We're going to the big city. Aren't you excited?"

"I am, actually." She grinned. "I can't wait to shop!"

"Shop!" I laughed. "Is that all you think about?"

"What else is there to do in New York City?" She raised her eyebrows.

"I can't wait to see the Statue of Liberty. I'm going to run up all the steps!" I pointed out Nate's jeep as it pulled up. "Ready?"

"You do realize that there's an elevator?" Kelsie tagged along behind me. "Wait, there is an elevator, right?"

With Maby already perched in the front seat—looking as fantastic as ever—I settled into the backseat beside Kelsie. Nate blasted the radio and we took off.

It didn't take long for me to realize that Nate and I had the same taste in music. Soon we were shouting at each other over the wind and the radio about the different songs that we loved.

As we neared the city, I began to get even more excited. Nothing could ruin a day like this, not even Maby's turning down the radio and complaining of a headache.

"I figured we'd visit Lady Liberty first." Nate navigated into a parking spot, then smiled as he glanced back at me. "Sound good to you?"

"Absolutely!"

"I can't wait to check out the gift shop." Kelsie climbed out of the jeep.

"Me too!" Maby grinned. "I did some pre-shopping online. I hope they have everything I want."

"I'm sure they will." Kelsie fell into step beside her. "I've read that they're very good at keeping the place stocked up."

"I hadn't really thought about the gift shop." I shrugged as I naturally matched Nate's pace. "Thank you so much for driving and for spending the day with us."

"Don't thank me yet." He grinned. "Thank me after you have a great day."

"Oh, I already know it's going to be a great day." I started for the steps. "Especially since I'm going to beat you to the top!"

"Are you sure you want to challenge me?" Nate grabbed me around the waist just before I could reach the steps and swung me out of the way. As he mounted the first step, he looked back at me and laughed.

"Cheater!" I shrieked and tugged him back out of the way.

As I charged up the steps, I could hear him right behind me. I could also hear Kelsie asking for the elevator.

My heart pounded as I climbed as fast as I could. Even though I wanted to be the first to the top, hearing Nate right behind me actually thrilled me. I loved that he could keep up with me and that he didn't mind if I managed to go just a little faster than him.

As we emerged from the top of the stairs, I stumbled over the last step and started to fall forward.

"No you don't!" He caught me from behind and pulled me back against him. His warm voice drifted over my shoulder as he steadied me. "I guess we'll have to call this one a tie."

EIGHTEEN

I laughed as I pulled away from him. "There's still the way down."

"Can I catch my breath first?" He gulped down a few deep breaths as he turned to look at the view.

I followed his gaze, my breath catching in my throat. In all the excitement of racing to the top, I'd forgotten what we'd come here to see. I stepped up beside him, my heart pounding as I soaked in the sight that I never thought I'd have the chance to see.

Despite how much I missed my family, in that moment, I fell in love with New York City. I fell in love with the outstretched water. I fell in love with the moment, one that felt like a dream.

Nate's pinky finger grazed against mine. The subtle tingle that shot through me took my breath away again. I blinked, then focused on the view again as I slid my hands into my pockets.

"We should get back." I cleared my throat. "Kelsie and Maby are probably wondering where we are." I winced at the thought of how angry Maby might be that I'd spent so much time alone with Nate.

He turned toward me as I continued to look at the view.

"Jaxx." He brushed my long ponytail back from my shoulder and leaned a little closer to me. "I'm so glad that we got to do this together. You're always up for anything. It makes everything more fun."

"I feel the same way." I shot him a quick smile. "I'm glad I have you to go on adventures with—and to beat down the steps." I gave him a light push and headed for the stairs.

"Now who's cheating?" he hollered as he chased after me.

As I ran down each step my heart pounded harder. Maybe I'd gotten a bit out of shape. With Nate right behind me, it was hard to catch my breath. As much as I wanted to beat him, I realized that I also didn't want to leave him behind.

I stepped down off the last step and found Maby and Kelsie near the entrance in the middle of a burst of laughter. I froze as Maby looked in my direction.

"Oof!" Nate bumped into me as he came off of the last step.

"Sorry." I stepped aside as he laughed.

"I'm the one that should be apologizing. I can't believe you beat me again." He groaned.

"The race to the top was a tie, remember?" I smiled at him, then glanced at Maby.

As I feared, her laughter had disappeared and her expression hardened.

"Let's go eat." Kelsie smiled as she held up a few bags from the gift shop. "I've gotten what I came here for."

"Just give me a second, I want to find something for my sister." I headed toward the gift shop and hoped that no one would follow me.

My heart continued to race and it left me unsettled. I needed to find a way to calm down.

As I browsed through souvenirs, I thought about how much I already loved New York City. The thought of leaving it brought up a sense of dread. I ran my fingers across a tiny statue replica and smiled at the thought of its being on my sister's desk. Lucy would love it. I grabbed it, a magnet for my mother, and a keychain for my father and walked up to the register.

"Good choices." Nate smiled as he walked up beside me.

"You're not getting anything?" I looked at his empty hands.

"No, I've got more souvenirs than I'll ever need." He laughed. "But I'll never get tired of coming here. What did you think of the view?"

"It was amazing." I took the bag from the cashier then followed Nate out of the shop. "I just love it here."

"I'm glad you do. Not everyone likes it. Some people just like to visit." He shrugged.

"I can't imagine leaving." I frowned as we joined up with Kelsie and Maby and headed for a restaurant.

"Are you going to?" He looked over at me, his brow furrowed. "Leave at the end of summer, I mean?"

"I'm not sure yet." I took a deep breath, then released it as we stepped into the restaurant.

Once our food was ordered, I did my best to remain quiet. I didn't want to say or do anything to upset Maby more than I already had. But it wasn't too hard as she and Kelsie chatted away about everything under the sun. It seemed to me that Kelsie was having more fun with Maby than I had seen her have in a long time.

"What about you?" I looked across the table at Nate. "What are you going to do after summer?"

"I'll be going back to NYU." He smiled. "I've got a few more years to go."

"And I'll be starting," Maby piped up with a proud smile. "I just graduated from Oak Brook Academy. It's a boarding school here." She smiled at Nate. "So, I'll be joining him at the end of summer. He's promised to show me the ropes. Right, Nate?"

"Of course." He grinned at her. "I would never leave you hanging, Maby. You're going to love it."

"I can't wait." She grinned, then looked directly at me. "What college are you going to, Jaxx?"

"Uh—I'm taking some time off." I glanced away from her. I wasn't about to admit that I hadn't actually applied to any. The thought of going to college right after graduating made me sick to my stomach. I wanted a little freedom.

"I did that when I graduated." Nate nodded. "It was the best thing I ever did. It gave me a break. I did a lot of surfing." He laughed. "It was the best year. I'm sure you'll have a lot of fun."

"What about you, Kelsie?" Maby spoke up before Nate could say anything more. "Are you going to take a year off too? Or are you going to get started on your future?"

NINETEEN

I felt the sharpness in Maby's tone. I knew it was meant to dig at me.

But I took a breath and ignored it. The thought of spending a year surfing, especially if I got to do it with Nate, thrilled me.

"Actually, I've been considering sticking around New York." Kelsie took a sip of her drink, then smiled at me. "If I can convince Jaxx to do it too."

"You have?" My eyes widened as I looked at her. "Since when?"

"Since I overheard Patti and Hannah discussing keeping us on for the year. We'd go back to the city with them. Patti hasn't come out and offered it, but I think they're going to." She grinned. "Wouldn't that be great?"

"Yes!" I blurted out the word as my heart jumped at the thought. "But I'm not sure." I sat back in my chair. "That's a long time to be away from home."

"Sure it is." Maby nodded. "I mean, I've been living in boarding schools my whole life, so I'm used to being away from my family, but I guess for someone like you, it would be hard.

Plus, it's not like being out here on the beach. The city is much more fast-paced with no beaches to enjoy."

"That's not true." Nate shook his head. "There are so many places to go, museums to see, it's pretty great all year round." He met my eyes. "You should stay, Jaxx."

"We don't even know for sure that they're going to offer it to us." I shrugged as I looked back down at my food. A part of me really hoped that Hannah would offer for me to stay on after the summer, but it also felt a little scary.

I looked up at Maby as she and Nate shared a laugh over an inside joke. What must it have been like for her to spend so much time away from her family?

"You and Nate have been friends for a long time?" I smiled as she fluttered her hand against his shoulder.

"Oh yes." She sighed. "I met him during the summer after my first year at Oak Brook. He showed me how to really enjoy the Hamptons. He also showed me all around the city. Didn't you, Nate?" She stared into his eyes. "Do you remember our first time at the Statue of Liberty?"

"Yes." His cheeks flushed as he looked away from her. "That was a great day."

"We had so many." Maby leaned closer to him. "I don't think I would have enjoyed New York nearly as much without you around."

"You can survive anything, Maby." He stared straight into her eyes. "You're one of the strongest people I know."

As I sensed the genuine admiration in his tone, I realized that they had shared quite an adventure. Maby struck me as snippy and a bit jealous, but he saw something quite different in her. If I was honest, I could see why. She was confident, intelligent, and beautiful. Maybe if I'd spent so much time away from my family, I'd be a bit snippy too.

On the drive home from the city, Nate dropped Maby off

first at an apartment she shared with a few of her friends from Oak Brook. She leaned across the seat and gave Nate a warm hug.

"Thanks for letting me tag along. I had a great time." She looked into the backseat and waved to Kelsie and me, then headed for the apartment.

As Nate turned up the music, I lost myself in a fantasy about staying in New York. The more I thought about it, the more I liked the idea.

As he pulled up in front of the house to drop us both off, I woke from my thoughts and noticed that he'd been speaking to me for a few seconds.

"Huh? Sorry, I was a little lost in my head."

"It's okay. I was just saying it's still pretty warm out and that water looks gorgeous. Do you two want to go for a swim?" He glanced over at Kelsie.

"No way." Kelsie gathered up her shopping bags. "I had my exercise for the day, now I need a nap."

"A swim sounds great." I stretched as I stepped out of the jeep.

"I'll meet you out there in thirty minutes?" He met my eyes as I walked around the front of the jeep.

"I'll be there." I flashed him a smile, then followed Kelsie up onto the front porch. "I thought you were tired? Aren't you going home?" I leaned against the railing as Nate drove away.

"Yes, I'm exhausted, but I need to talk to you." She grabbed my hands and pulled me over to the porch swing. As we sat down, she looked into my eyes. "It's about Maby."

"You two seemed to get pretty buddy-buddy." I raised my eyebrows.

"We did. At first I was just trying to figure out what her intentions were, but the more time I spent with her, the more I realized she's a pretty nice person."

"Well, she definitely doesn't like me." I frowned.

"It's nothing personal." Kelsie sighed. "It's Nate."

"Nate?"

"She's got a thing for him, and she's convinced that he's into you." Kelsie shrugged. "They've been friends for a long time, and she was hoping they'd become something more this summer."

"Ugh. This is so stupid." I rolled my eyes. "She has no reason to be jealous over me. Did you tell her that?"

"No." Kelsie met my eyes. "I couldn't. Because I don't believe it."

"What? Why not?" I stood up from the porch swing. "I've told you, there's nothing between us!"

"You might feel that way, but Nate doesn't." Kelsie looked up at me. "I don't know how you can be so blind, Jaxx. He's obviously into you. Maby has been trying to distract him, but he's always focused on you."

"Because we're friends." I crossed my arms. "If she liked the same music as him, or wanted to surf, or do anything other than shop, maybe he'd be focused on her instead! Look, I don't want to come between her and Nate. I'll take care of this today."

"Jaxx." She took my hand as she stood up. "Please, just think about it. Make sure that's what you really want." She frowned as she studied me. "I'd hate to see you miss out on something wonderful."

"I have to get in my suit." I pulled my hand away from hers and ran into the house.

I loved Kelsie, but her insistence that Nate and I might have something between us drove me crazy. Now that I knew for sure why Maby had a problem with me, I hoped I could fix it all by making things clear with Nate. It might be a little embarrassing —since I knew he only saw me as a friend—but it had to be done.

TWENTY

After changing into my bathing suit, I walked back out to the porch to find Kelsie gone. I felt a pang of guilt as I wondered if I'd been too harsh with her. Of course we'd had our fights over the years, but generally we never had anything but love for one another. I took a deep breath as I considered why I'd reacted so defensively.

Kelsie was always trying to fix me up with people. It wasn't a new thing. But for some reason, with Nate it bothered me. I guessed it was because he was the best friend I'd made since arriving in the Hamptons, and I really didn't want anything messing that up—including Maby.

As I jogged out to the beach to meet Nate, I felt a rush of excitement. It had been a great day, and also a strange day. Now, armed with the knowledge that Maby had a huge crush on Nate, I felt prepared to put an end to all of the tension that she'd been throwing my way.

I could easily see the two of them together. They'd been friends for so long—their romance would be a sweet one. I just had to find a way to convince Maby that I was not a threat to her.

I dug my toes into the wet sand at the edge of the water and felt the wave suck it away from my feet. The sensation was fascinating, if not a little frightening. I thoughts about how it had felt to be pulled further and further from the shore. The memory left my stomach in knots.

"Beautiful." He spoke up from just behind me.

I looked up at the sky, painted with all the colors of the fading sunset, and smiled. "Yes, it is."

He stepped up beside me and released a slow breath. "Sometimes I get so lost in the beauty of things." He glanced over at me. "Sometimes I just wonder how it is even possible for them to exist."

"I've thought the same thing before." I met his eyes as I smiled. "I have to wonder—is it even real?"

"Exactly." He brushed a bit of sand from my cheek. "Jaxx, can we talk?"

"Sure, if you want. But, you have to catch me first!" I laughed as I splashed some water against his shins with my foot, then took off at a sprint across the sand.

"Oh you're going to pay for that!" He laughed as he chased after me.

I loved the way the sand sprayed out from beneath my feet and the splash as I ran along the edge of the water. I could sense him right behind me, his laughter light and musical in my ears. For an instant, I wondered how I'd gotten through life before I'd known him.

It was an odd thought, but at the same time, it made sense to me.

I slowed down and turned to face him, ankle deep in the water.

He stopped right in front of me, his toes sinking into the same sand as mine, as he tried to catch his breath.

For a long moment we stared into each other's eyes, too

winded to talk. As the waves tugged the sand out from under my feet, my heart raced. I felt a surge of something I couldn't identify flow through me. It was like the adrenaline after a fierce run, only more intense than I'd ever experienced. Stunned, I decided to burn it off in the water.

I turned and charged into the waves.

I heard him splash after me. Seconds later we were splashing and swimming through the waves.

"Let me show you something." He swam beside me. "There's a trick to diving through the waves—so they won't knock you around. Plus, they'll take you for a little ride." He grinned. "Just watch me."

I hung back a short distance and watched as he dove right into the rise of the wave. As it crashed over me, I felt his hand brush against mine, then curl around it as he tugged me back to the surface.

"I was okay." I sputtered as I wiped water from my eyes.

"I know." He smiled. "Your turn." He tipped his head toward a large wave that rolled in our direction. "Don't hesitate. Just go for it."

I took a deep breath as I recalled the sensation of being pulled out to sea. A quick glance at Nate reassured me that I wasn't alone. He wouldn't let me drift away. I faced the wave and launched myself right into the curl of it. The water lifted my body higher than I expected.

I laughed as I broke through the surface.

"Wow!"

"Right?" Nate grinned as he swam up beside me.

Before I could say another word, he disappeared into the next wave. I followed after him.

By the time we made our way to the shore, moonlight pooled across the surface of the sea. My legs and arms ached as I followed him toward a long piece of driftwood that stretched across the sand.

"That was so much fun, but I'm worn out."

"Sit." He gestured to the wood, then sat down on one side of it.

I sat down beside him and rested my arms on my knees. "Thanks, Nate. That was great."

"For me too." He tilted his head and met my eyes. "I figured that I owed it to you. I know that Maby was a little rough on you today."

"It's alright." I shrugged and dug my toes into the sand. "I still had a great day. I think my favorite part was the Statue of Liberty."

"Mine too." He held my gaze as he smiled. "That was an amazing moment, wasn't it? I'm so glad I got to share it with you."

"It was nice." I raised my eyebrows. "But it sounded like you had a pretty special moment with Maby there too."

"Right." He pushed his wet hair back from his eyes and sighed. "We kissed."

"It must have been so romantic." I leaned my shoulder against his. "How did you let her get away?"

"It's not like that." His voice hardened some. "When I first met Maby, she was so alone. I kind of felt the same way. We connected. But not like that." He looked out over the water. "She's been a great friend, and I would do anything to protect her. But something is just missing between us. It's never been there." He looked back at me, his eyes locked to mine. "I can't talk to her, not the way I talk to you. Jaxx, you make everything an adventure. I can't wait to see what happens next."

"Maybe you just haven't given her a chance." I looked down at the sand between my feet. "She seems sweet and it sounds like she's had things pretty rough. She's definitely your type."

"My type?" He whispered the words.

"I mean, it seems like you two would get along. She's beautiful. What are you waiting for?" I looked up at him again, our eyes locked, and my heart skipped a beat.

Why did I regret every word I'd just said? What was that heavy weight that had formed in the center of my chest?

TWENTY-ONE

I opened my eyes the next morning with that same weight on my chest. I kept hearing my own words play through my mind. I couldn't forget the strange look in Nate's eyes as he stared back at me. Seconds later he had taken off for the night.

Left alone on the beach, I'd tried to ignore the awful dread that seemed to be building within me. It felt just like the moment when the current tugged me further from the shore. It felt as if I might never find land again. It didn't make any sense.

I tried to wash it off in the shower, then decided to go for a run on the beach.

As I ran across the sand, I focused on the beach house ahead of me—the one I knew Nate lived in. As I neared it, I felt a billow of hope that he might be out on the deck, maybe even waiting for me. A good race would help clear things up for me, I was sure.

But the deck was empty.

I paused to fiddle with my phone for a moment and glanced toward the tall glass windows that overlooked the deck.

Nothing.

Disappointed, I began to run again. I had the day off and I

had hoped that he might offer another surfing lesson. But the way he'd left the night before—it didn't seem as if he was eager to teach me anything.

Had I said something wrong? Was it just my imagination?

When I returned from my run I decided to bite the bullet and send him a text. I'd probably gotten the wrong impression the night before and was overthinking everything. I could do that when something made me nervous.

I sent him a text asking if we could get together since I had the day free.

As I waited for him to text back, I sent Kelsie a text as well asking if she had any plans for the day.

My phone buzzed the moment I put it down. I thought it would be Kelsie replying, but instead it was Nate. I stared down at his words.

SORRY, I can't. Busy today.

IT WAS A SIMPLE TEXT. But something about it felt cold. As if he'd used as few words as possible.

Again I pushed the thought from my mind. It had been such a good day yesterday and at the same time it had come to such a strange ending. Everyone had an off day. Maybe Nate just needed a break.

Seconds later Kelsie called.

"Morning." I did my best to sound cheerful.

"How was your swim last night?" Her voice had a suggestive tone.

"Stop!" I sighed as a bit of anger spiked inside of me. "Please, Kelsie, can you stop doing that? I know that you mean well, but things got weird between Nate and me last night and now thanks to all these ideas you're putting in my head, I can't stop thinking about it."

"Oh, I'm sorry." Kelsie paused. "Weird how? Did you kiss him?"

"Kelsie!" I groaned.

"Okay, I promise—not a word about Nate—or the kiss."

"There was no kiss!" My cheeks heated at the thought. My heart skipped a beat. That weight returned in the center of my chest. "Can we do something together today?"

"Of course. I'd love to spend the day with you. We'll do some shopping and some eating and some more shopping. Sound good?"

I didn't have the heart to tell her that the only part I looked forward to was the eating, but at the moment anything was better than over-analyzing Nate's text.

"Okay, sounds good. I'd love to hit that cafe again on the beach. I really liked the food there and I want to try something else on the menu." I felt some relief as I focused on something other than Nate.

"Great, see you soon. I promise, I'll be good." She hung up the phone.

I hoped she meant it. My emotions were all over the place in a way that I wasn't used to. I felt as if I should apologize to Nate, but I had no idea what I might have done wrong.

I stepped out onto the front porch to wait for Kelsie. No matter what, I had to shake this mood off. I wouldn't let it ruin my day and especially not my friendship with Nate.

"Jaxx, over here!" Kelsie waved to me from the sidewalk.

"What is that?" I laughed as I stared at the tandem bicycle she had.

"Something fun!" She grinned. "You can't beat me on this, can you?" She patted the seat behind her. "Hop on, we have lots of shops to hit!"

I rolled my eyes but couldn't help but laugh as I mounted the bicycle. It did distract me. Kelsie's chatter about Lance distracted me too as we stopped by shop after shop.

By the time we arrived at the cafe, I'd nearly forgotten about all the strange feelings I'd been experiencing. We parked our tandem bicycle out front, then headed inside the cafe.

Moments after we took our order out onto the patio that overlooked the beach, I heard a familiar laugh. It took only a second for me to spot Nate in a group of people just beyond the patio on the beach.

"Hey, Nate!" I smiled and waved to him.

I noticed Maby beside him and then she waved to us.

Nate stared at me for a moment, then offered a smile as he nodded to us.

A nod? I waited for him to come over and say hello.

He turned his attention back to the others he'd been talking to.

"Aren't you going to go over and say hi?" Kelsie nudged my shoulder.

"Isn't that what I just did?" I frowned as I looked back at my food.

"I guess." Kelsie patted the back of my hand. "Maybe you're the one acting weird, hon."

"Maybe I am." I glanced up again, just in time to see Nate look away from me.

Heaviness filled my chest. Yes, it could have been my imagination, but as he walked away with his friends around him, I noticed that he didn't look back.

TWENTY-TWO

"Slow down, kiddo!" I laughed as Bella plowed into me with a bucket of water and a body covered in sand.

"Bury me, Jaxx!" she pleaded as the water spilled out into the sand.

"Okay, okay." I playfully tackled her into the sand, then began to cover her feet and legs with it.

"Oh boy, they are going to need baths before we go out to dinner!" Hannah called from the beach chair she lounged on beside Patti.

"I think we all are." Patti brushed off a bit of sand that Cherish had piled on her stomach. "These kids are going to bring all of their sand back to the city with them when the summer is over."

The mention of the summer coming to an end inspired the heavy weight in my chest again. The season had barely started, but the thought of it ending sent a chill down my spine. I wasn't sure why.

"Hey, there's Nate." Kelsie nudged my toe with her foot. "He's over there." She pointed to a group near the lifeguard stand.

I saw Nate, laughing as usual, right beside Maby. As I waved to him, he nodded, then waved back with a light smile.

Something felt off about it. I took a deep breath and glanced at Kelsie.

"Aren't you going to go over and talk to him?" Kelsie smiled. "I'm sure he's eager to see you."

"I'm not so sure about that." I frowned.

"Go on, I'll keep an eye on the kids while you do. You can't keep waiting to find out. If you think something is strange between the two of you, just go ask him about it. I'm sure you'll clear things right up. Then you can stop pouting so much."

"Pouting?" I glared at her. "I haven't been pouting."

"Well, you haven't been yourself either." She tipped her head toward Nate. "Just go have a quick chat. What harm could it do?"

I stood up from the sand and brushed some from the backs of my thighs. What harm could it do? It could mean my whole summer was ruined, although I wasn't sure why or how. It could mean that the best friend I'd made in the Hamptons, for some reason, didn't want much to do with me anymore.

As I walked over, Nate met my eyes, then glanced away.

That was it right there. Never once had he looked at me without smiling or waving me over. Why did he act like I was the last person he wanted to see?

"Hi, Nate." I paused beside him. Most of his friends had scattered, but I saw Maby nearby. I felt a pang of guilt, knowing that she thought he had a thing for me and that my being near him probably made her feel insecure. But my intentions were good. I just wanted my friend back.

"Hey, how's it going?" He smiled at me as he met my eyes again. "It looks like you're having fun over there."

"Always a blast with those kids." I laughed and shook my head. "How are you doing?"

"Alright. Just trying to enjoy the sunshine while it lasts." He looked out over the water, then back at me.

"Have you been out surfing?" Awkwardness swelled within me as I waited for his response. Why was he taking so long to answer?

"A bit." He cleared his throat.

"I'd love another lesson sometime—if you don't mind, I mean." I shrugged and looked out over the water as well.

"Sure, of course. Whenever." He shrugged.

"Are you free anytime soon?" I looked back at him. His tone wasn't as warm as usual. But he smiled, and he didn't try to walk away from me.

"I'm a little busy. But I'll let you know." He looked past me, at a boy in the distance. "Hey! Conner!" He took off at a run to catch up with Conner.

Left alone, I stared after him. He'd said all the right things. He'd been kind. He'd been friendly. But things were definitely not right. My stomach churned with the thought that maybe I really had lost him.

As I trudged back across the sand to join Kelsie and the kids, she looked up at me with a small frown.

"Didn't go well, huh?"

"I just don't know what is going on." I dropped down beside her and frowned. "Maybe he's just tired of me."

"Maybe he's just distracted." Kelsie smiled. "The summer can get pretty busy, right? I'm sure he's just spacing out a bit. He'll be back to normal in no time."

"Maybe." I smiled at her as we began to gather the toys up. "No matter what, we have each other, right?"

"Oh sure, but Lance does have a friend you might like." She grinned as I threw a bucket at her.

"Easy now, you haven't even seen him yet!"

"I don't care what he looks like. That's not what I'm here for." I groaned.

"I know, you're here for Nate." She fluttered her eyelashes.

"Kelsie!" I bit back the words I wanted to say as three kids looked up at me with wide eyes, startled by my shout.

"Everything okay, girls?" Hannah lowered her sunglasses as she looked at us. "I want things to go smoothly for my birthday dinner tonight, alright?"

"Sorry, Hannah." I flashed her a smile. "Kelsie is just teasing me." I looked back at Kelsie with a stern glare.

"Sorry." She stepped closer to me and lowered her voice. "Although I don't think you'd be getting so mad if there wasn't something going on there."

"I'm mad because you keep acting like there's something between me and Nate, but there isn't. I told him to give Maby a chance, because I want him to be happy—and I want Maby to be happy. But now all I really want is my friend back. Instead, he's acting weird, and I can only guess that Maby has something to do with it. She doesn't want him talking to me anymore or something."

"You told him that?" Kelsie stared at me, her mouth half-open.

"Yes." I stared back at her. "So?"

"So maybe you need to think things through a little more. I don't think Maby would do that. She's definitely interested in him, but she wouldn't ruin your friendship to get him. She's not like that." She raised her eyebrows, then waved to Patti, who was urging us both to get packed up. "We'll be right there!"

I finished collecting the toys, still annoyed. What had been so wrong with what I'd said to Nate?

TWENTY-THREE

Wrangling two kids at a restaurant wasn't exactly my idea of a fun night, but the restaurant itself thrilled me. It had so much history, and as Hannah rattled off the names of celebrities that had eaten there, I could almost picture them seated at the tables around me. I could certainly get used to living in a place with so much glamour.

Hannah still hadn't mentioned anything about me staying on after the summer. Now that things were so awkward with Nate, I wasn't sure that I really wanted to stay. He'd talked so highly of the city, but would it be the same if I didn't get to share those things with him?

"Excuse me, I'm just going to use the restroom." I stood up from the table. "I won't be gone long, I promise."

"Don't worry, I can keep them all coloring." Kelsie slid into my chair and helped all three kids to pick out new crayons.

As I hurried to the restroom, I glanced back to be sure that they were all still seated. In the same moment that I looked back, I collided with someone. I turned back with a gasp.

"I'm so sorry, I wasn't paying attention."

"It's alright." Maby smiled as she folded her arms across her stomach and settled her confident gaze on me. "I'm sure you're busy with the kids."

"Maby." I stepped aside. "I'm really sorry. I hope I didn't wrinkle your dress."

Her dress. Her gorgeous dress that showed off her figure while remaining classy and alluring all at the same time. How did she manage to pull that off? I could easily see why Nate would be interested in her.

"My dress is fine, thanks." She smoothed it down, then looked back at me. "It's good to see you."

"You too." I smiled again, then continued on to the restroom.

As I stepped inside, I caught a glimpse of myself in the mirror. Sure, my body was toned from all the sports that I played, but it was hidden with my loose top and straight-legged pants. The same old ponytail hung down my back. I looked all of twelve, with my face bare of any make-up.

As I compared myself to Maby, I realized that there was an art to the way she looked. She knew what would flatter her figure, she knew how to design a smoky eye, and she knew what shade of lipstick to use.

That knowledge just wasn't in me.

I looked away from my reflection and tried not to think about it. I didn't want to be like Maby or even Kelsie. I told myself that again and again. Sure, they got plenty of attention, but I didn't want a guy to be interested in me just because of the way I looked. I wanted him to be interested in me because of who I was.

As I walked back to the table, I caught sight of Maby seated at another table, not far from mine. She had her back to me. Seated across from her, dressed in a tailored suit that accentuated his muscular frame, Nate laughed in response to something she said.

I felt a sudden ripple of fear that maybe he was laughing at something she'd said about me. I pushed the thought away. Nate would never make fun of me. He wouldn't make fun of anyone. He wasn't that kind of person.

My heart pounded as I wondered if I could make it back to the table without him spotting me.

Too late.

He lifted his hand in a wave. "Hey, Jaxx!"

I took a deep breath and walked toward the table. "Nate." I smiled at him as I paused beside the table. "I just ran into Maby, I didn't realize you two were here together."

"Yes—together." Maby brushed her hair back from her eyes as she tilted her head to look at me. "It's one of our favorite restaurants, isn't it, Nate?"

"Eh, it's a little classy for me." He tugged at his tie then shrugged. "But it's nice to get dressed up once in a while."

I bit into my bottom lip as I felt his gaze wander over my simple outfit. An awkward second drew itself out for what felt like a century.

"Well, I should let you two get back to your meal." I backed away from the table, eager to escape Nate's probing gaze.

"Good to see you, Jaxx."

His words followed me to the table.

Kelsie met my eyes with a wince. "I didn't even know they were here until he called you over. How did that go?"

"Strange. It was strange." I sat back down in my chair and focused on the two kids, who both wanted my attention.

I couldn't help but steal a few glances back over at Nate and Maby as they shared their meal. He seemed to be laughing quite a lot. She leaned across to dab some sauce from his chin with her cloth napkin. They looked like they'd been together for years.

My stomach twisted so tight that I couldn't imagine taking a bite of food. When I watched them stand up to leave, I saw him take her arm. His fingers wrapped around it so casually, as if he'd been born to hold onto her.

My heart dropped as they moved past our table without so much as a word.

"Jaxx?" Kelsie nudged my foot with her own. "They're bringing Hannah's cake out."

"Oh, okay." I turned my attention to the celebration.

I smiled, cheered, and wished Hannah a wonderful birthday, but none of the festivities lifted the heavy weight that had settled on my chest. I couldn't quite understand the feeling, but as I watched Hannah lean in close to kiss her husband, the romantic gesture sparked something in me.

Something I hadn't expected. Something I wasn't sure that I was ready to believe.

TWENTY-FOUR

I sunk my toes deep into the sand and let the warm breeze off the water tickle across my face. I'd fled to the beach as soon as the kids were in bed. I needed some time to think about everything that had happened at the restaurant. Although it didn't seem like much on the surface, underneath, everything was in chaos.

My heart pounded, my chest ached, my palms were covered in sweat. Every other second the memory of Maby and Nate together at the restaurant flashed into my mind.

But why?

I looked out over the water as I began to walk across the sand again. Why did it bother me so much that they were together—that they had obviously been on a date? I didn't care who Nate dated.

In fact, I'd come to like Maby through what both Nate and Kelsie had shared about her. So why wasn't I happy to see them together?

Was I just jealous that he seemed to be spending so much time with her instead of surfing or hanging out with me? I could remember a few male friends in high school that I'd lost the moment they started dating someone. The girls didn't like the idea of them hanging out with me. Maybe that was what I was afraid of?

I closed my eyes for a moment and thought about Nate chasing after me along the shore. I remembered his arms around me, as we'd fallen into the sand.

My heart fluttered. The weight lifted for just a second.

My eyes snapped open and I took a deep breath. I looked out over the water as I remembered the first day we'd met. I'd been ready to give up, so exhausted, and then he was there. He brought me to shore and didn't tease me for my failure to navigate the water. From that moment on, he'd supported me at every turn.

I drew another breath as I remembered what it was like to dive through the waves with him.

My heart fluttered again. That weight lifted again.

"Oh no." The words slipped past my lips as I waded into the water and felt the sand tugged out from under my feet.

I knew what the chaos inside of me meant. It wasn't just that I was jealous over him spending more time with Maby. It was that I was jealous over him spending any time at all with her romantically.

My cheeks flushed and my mind spun as I recalled all those moments that he'd made an effort to be close to me—the way he always said something kind to me. He wasn't just like any other guy friend I'd ever had. He was different.

He wasn't insulted when I did better than him at something. He didn't demand that I act a certain way in order to be around him. He seemed to be genuinely interested in who I was as a person.

I swam out into the water, the waves mild as they sloshed across my skin. The moon had begun to rise in the sky. It created a silvery path across the water, straight toward me.

In that moment, I would have given anything to have Nate right there beside me.

I didn't want to be his friend. I pursed my lips as I closed my eyes. I didn't want to just learn how to surf from him. I didn't want to just race on the beach.

A jolt of fear carried through me as I dared to allow myself to imagine what it would be like if he swam up beside me right in that moment. I could feel his fingertips graze along my arm. I could hear his laughter just beside me. I could sense his beautiful eyes settled on me—looking deep into mine.

"Nate." I whispered his name as I continued to face the truth.

I didn't want him to be interested in Maby. I didn't want him to date her or kiss her or spend his time with her.

I wanted all of that for myself.

I shivered as the water grew cooler. But the thought of him leaning in to kiss me filled me with warmth, despite the temperature of the water. My heart raced and every cell in my body pulsated with the desire to find out what it would really be like to share an intimate moment with him.

Never in my life had I wanted to kiss someone so badly.

Even the boys I did kiss didn't create this magical desire within me. It was beyond anything I had ever experienced before. The thought of not being able to be with him created that same sensation within me that the sand running out from under my feet did—that the strong current of the waves did. I couldn't imagine what it would be like never to get to be with him.

Startled by my discovery, I swam back to shore.

"It doesn't matter." I broke into a run as I tried to push the thoughts from my mind. "It doesn't matter what I think I want. It's never going to happen and I need to let it go."

Those words sent daggers through my heart. But I knew they were true.

Nate liked girls like Maby. Maby, who was perfect and knew exactly what to wear and how to wear it. Maby who could eat at a fancy restaurant without feeling awkward.

He liked girls like Kelsie, who knew how to turn on the charm whenever she wanted to. Girls that wouldn't be awkward or strange. Girls that would know when they actually had feelings for someone, instead of pushing that person toward someone else.

"It's too late." I drew in heavy breaths as I finally stopped running. "He's already with Maby. He's already with the person he's probably meant to be with."

TWENTY-FIVE

Sitting on the edge of my bed, I stared at my phone on the table beside me. I had plugged it in and turned it off in an attempt to resist the urge that built within me during my walk back to the house. My heart pounded in my chest, and with every breath I took, new feelings surged through me.

How had I been so blind? The entire time I'd protested Kelsie's teasing, I had been getting to know Nate more and more. I had no idea that I was falling for him. I still didn't know exactly how it had happened. But I did know that it was like nothing I'd ever felt before.

I stood up and turned my back to the phone. "I shouldn't text him. I shouldn't call him. I shouldn't even think about him."

I pressed my hands against my face as a wave of dizziness washed over me. The thought of never speaking to him again— the thought of never telling him how I really felt—made every muscle in my body weak. I couldn't imagine going another minute without getting my feelings out.

I fell back on my bed and groaned as I remembered the way that Kelsie had looked at me when I told her that I'd sent Nate off to be with Maby. Of course, she could clearly see that I was being an idiot. Why hadn't I seen that?

My mind flashed back to the two of them at dinner. Had it been a date? They hadn't exactly been sitting close. They hadn't been holding hands. Nate didn't seem to mind when I'd walked over to say hello. Was it possible that they were just out as friends?

"No way, not at a fancy restaurant like that." I frowned at the thought. I wouldn't have even thought about taking Nate to a place like that.

Because I wasn't Maby. Because I didn't know how to be someone like that.

But what if I was? Or what if I could at least pretend to be?

My heart raced at the thought of Nate seeing me the way that he saw Maby. What if he didn't see his friend, Jaxx, but instead saw a girl that he could date?

"It's too late." I shook my head. "It's too late, I just have to stop thinking about it."

But was it?

My competitive nature sparked deep inside of me. I wasn't used to giving up. I always enjoyed a challenge. Maybe Nate had his eyes set on Maby, but that didn't mean he couldn't notice me too. All I had to do was show him that I was an option and maybe he would see that he felt the same way about me.

I thought about the things he'd said to me on the beach the night I'd told him to give Maby a chance. He certainly seemed to enjoy my company. Was it possible that he had some kind of interest in me too?

If so, I couldn't let him slip away without at least trying to make something happen between us.

I picked up my phone and turned it back on. As my fingers hovered over the keypad, I wondered if he'd even be home. If they had been on a date, they'd most likely gone on to do something romantic after dinner. He might be kissing her right this second.

I winced and set the phone down. It would be wrong to interrupt, wouldn't it?

That heavy feeling threatened to cave in my chest. I closed my eyes and felt the tug of waves rushing back toward the ocean.

No, I couldn't give up—not without trying.

Before I could change my mind, I typed out a text. I had tomorrow off. It would be my chance to get his attention, to see if he felt the same way about me.

NATE, would you like to go to dinner with me tomorrow night?

I SENT the text before I could delete it.

As soon as it went through, my heart dropped. What had I just done? My heart raced as I wondered if he'd even text me back.

My thoughts spun as each second slipped by. Then I saw dots begin to bounce as he started to write a text back to me.

I held my breath. Would he say he was too busy? Would he wonder why I'd even asked?

As the text popped up, a mixture of relief and excitement burst through me.

SURE. Is it a special occasion?

THE QUESTION STRUCK me as a little odd. But then my invite had probably struck him as a little odd. I'd spent so much time pushing him away, that if he did have any interest in me, he'd probably given up by now.

I bit into my bottom lip as I considered how to respond. I didn't want to say too much. I didn't want to show my hand before I had the chance to change his mind.

Instead, I sent back a quick and simple text.

I HOPE SO.

THE DOTS on the screen began to bounce as he started to write something back. I watched them bounce, eagerly awaiting his next text.

But after a few seconds, they stopped and didn't start again.

What had he written that he'd decided not to send?

I pushed the worry away as I flopped back on my bed. It didn't matter. He'd said yes to dinner, which meant that I had one chance to show him that I could be more of a girly girl. I had one night to get him to see me the same way that he saw Maby— as an option, as someone he might like to have as more than a friend.

The idea sent a shower of sparks through me.

I closed my eyes and remembered his arms as they'd wrapped around me. Wouldn't it be amazing to actually be held by him—to look into his eyes as he leaned close to me, to know that it was me that he wanted to kiss?

But that would never happen if I didn't make sure that I turned into someone he could be attracted to. I couldn't do that without some help—or more accurately, a lot of help.

I sent another text, this time to Kelsie. I explained what I'd realized, what I'd done, and exactly the kind of help I needed.

Instantly she texted me back with a dozen emojis that I

couldn't quite decipher, followed by a promise to meet me first thing in the morning.

I wasn't quite sure what would happen next, but I knew I was going to try my hardest to become the type of girl that someone like Nate would want to be with.

TWENTY-SIX

Not long after I woke up, I heard a knock at the front door. With the family gone on a special outing, there was only me to answer. Still a bit sluggish from a fitful night's sleep, I climbed out of bed.

"Kelsie?" I laughed as I opened the door. "Don't you think it's a little early to start getting ready?"

"Not at all!" She lugged in a small suitcase as she pushed past me into the house.

"What did you bring?" My eyes widened as she set the suitcase on my bed.

"Oh wait, I forgot the garment bag." She rushed past me and back out the door.

"Kelsie?" I called after her as she grabbed a garment bag from the porch, then carried it into my room. "There's no way you need all this stuff."

"Oh, it's not for me." She grinned as she pushed me down to sit on the side of the bed. "Just look at you." She scrunched up her nose. "There's so much natural beauty to highlight. I'm not even sure where to start. Where are you two going to dinner?" She unzipped the garment bag and pulled out a few dresses.

"Oh, Kelsie I'm not sure any of those are going to work." I frowned as I looked from sequins to slit skirts to a body-hugging black dress.

"Why not?" She held up the black dress. "I think this will be perfect on you."

"I am going to need something dressy." I frowned as I looked over the dress. "I made a reservation at a really nice steak restaurant. It's definitely not my style, but after I saw him last night at Hannah's favorite restaurant, I realized that he's probably used to more expensive places."

"I'm just so happy you're doing this." She gave my ponytail a light tug. "He is going to be thrilled."

"I'm not so sure about that." I sighed as I ran my fingertips across the satiny smooth texture of the dress. "If he was on a date with Maby last night, then I'm probably too late."

"That was no date. They were just out together." She shook her head. "I would be able to tell if it was a date."

"Oh really?" I laughed as I looked up at her. "How?"

"I'd just know." She shrugged. "Besides, even Maby knows that he's into you. I don't think you have anything to worry about."

I wanted to believe her, but as I watched her pile make-up onto the bed beside me, my heart sank. Kelsie knew how to look the part—so did Maby. Someone as handsome and wonderful as Nate deserved to be with a girl who would look amazing on his arm.

"This was such a bad idea." I groaned. "What if I make a fool of myself?"

"You won't." Kelsie took my hand. "I'm not going to let you. I promise. Now just go try on the dress. We need to pick out which one you're going to wear before we start figuring out your hair."

"My hair." I reached up and touched the ponytail I always wore. "We're going to keep it up, right?"

"No way." Kelsie smiled, then held the dress out to me. "Go on, we're going to have to keep it moving."

I laughed at her again and headed for the bathroom with the dress. After trying on everything she'd brought, I realized hours had slipped by. Not only that, I was exhausted from changing the dresses over and over again. Every time I looked in the mirror, I felt like I was wearing a costume. Every time I tried something new on, Kelsie had to see me in the previous dress again.

"This is it." I huffed as I stepped out of the bathroom with the black dress on again. "I don't want to try anything else on. It's not the dresses. It's me. They just don't look right on me."

"Take your hair down." Kelsie crossed her arms as she studied my figure. "That dress hugs you in all the right places. You fill it out even better than I do. But I need to see it with your hair down."

I yanked the hairband out of my hair and felt it tumble against my shoulders and down my back.

"Wow." She took a step back as she stared at me. "Yes, you're absolutely right. This is it. This is the dress you are going to wear tonight."

"Are you sure?" I frowned. "I think it's too tight."

"It fits you perfectly." She turned me toward the mirror that hung on the back of my bedroom door. "Take a look."

I stared at my reflection. I thought I looked like I always did —only it was me wearing a dress.

"Straighten up." She gave my back a light swat.

I sighed as I straightened my shoulders and spine. The moment I did, the reflection in the mirror transformed. With my hair in waves over my shoulders and my chin lifted with pride, for the first time, I saw myself in a different light.

It lasted for just a second before fading away.

"I don't know, Kelsie." I squeezed my hands together.

"Sweetheart, that's the problem. If you want to look good in the dress, all you have to do is feel good in it. Having a little confidence goes a long way. I know you have it too. I see it in you when you challenge Nate to a race or play a sport. You exude confidence. But now you need to feel it when you're wearing this dress—with your hair down—when you walk into that restaurant to meet Nate." She gave my shoulder a pat. "Don't worry, once you feel it, it'll come naturally to you." She peered at me through the mirror. "Now, let's get started on that hair."

Kelsie spent the next few hours smoothing my hair out into a beautiful wave and adding make-up to my pre-moisturized face. It wasn't easy for me to sit still, but with each step I could see the improvement that she insisted would be there.

By the time she was done, I barely recognized my reflection. It wasn't that I looked all that different, it was that everything that I admired about myself had been accentuated. I'd never felt comfortable with my hair down, but as I studied the way it floated like a cloud over my shoulder—with the gentlest wave to it—I could see everything that Kelsie had described.

"Jaxx, you're gorgeous." Kelsie squeezed my shoulders as she smiled. "See?"

"I see." I smiled as I stared at my reflection in the mirror. "I see it took us all day to get me here too." I laughed.

"Stop joking around." Kelsie turned me around to face her. "Jaxx, I am so proud of you for doing this. You're going to blow Nate away tonight."

"I hope so." I murmured as I turned back to look again.

Was this the Jaxx that he wanted? Would it be enough?

TWENTY-SEVEN

I heard Nate's jeep pull up and my knees threatened to buckle.

What was I thinking? What if he took one look at me and laughed?

My stomach twisted at the thought. Why wouldn't he laugh? It was pretty absurd for me to suddenly invite him to dinner and dress up the way that I had.

But I knew Nate better than that. Even if he was amused, he wouldn't let it show. He wouldn't hurt my feelings. I was sure of that.

"There's no turning back now." I looked into the mirror one last time before I heard the knock on the front door.

It startled me. He'd always just waited in the jeep when he'd picked me up before.

With my heart in my throat, I walked to the door. My hand trembled as I turned the knob. Just before I pulled it open, I felt a rush.

The adrenaline of taking a shot right before the buzzer, the anticipation of approaching the finish line with my competitors right beside me—it rocketed through me and instantly released a burst of confidence. If I was going to win this race, I had to give it my all.

I straightened my shoulders and took a deep breath as I swung the door open.

"Jaxx?" Nate took a slight step back as he stared at me, his eyes wide and his mouth half-open. He blinked, then swept his gaze from my head to my toes before looking back up at me. "Wow—you look amazing." His voice faltered as he spoke.

Was he lying? I searched his eyes in an attempt to figure out his reaction.

"We should go, we're going to be late." Flustered, I stepped past him onto the porch.

"I feel a little underdressed." He caught up with me in time to open the passenger side door of the car. "Where exactly are we going?"

"You look great." I smiled at him as I looked over his button-down shirt and casual pants. It wasn't what he'd been wearing at the restaurant the night before, but it also wasn't jeans and a t-shirt. It crossed my mind that he might have dressed up for me. I pushed the thought away as I settled in the passenger seat. "You'll see. I'll tell you where to go."

"Jaxx?" He hesitated by my door and stared through the open window at me. "What is this all about?"

"You'll see." I cleared my throat and looked out through the windshield.

I couldn't tell him yet. Not when he still had the chance to beg off from dinner, not when he could let me down easy. I needed to put my best foot forward to show him that I could be like the type of girl he could fall for. It was the only way he would even consider me a possibility.

"Alright." He smiled as he walked around the front of the jeep.

I caught sight of the dimple in his cheek and the glimmer in his eyes. I guessed that he was curious to see what I had in mind.

As I instructed him on where to turn, I caught sight of that glimmer in his eyes more than once. He seemed to be thrilled to be on this adventure with me. But would he still feel that way when I told him the truth?

"Turn in right here." I pointed to the restaurant beside us.

"Here?" He slowly turned into the packed parking lot. "Why?" He glanced over at me, the glimmer fading.

"Just do what I ask." I sighed, then managed a smile. "Please?"

"Sure." He smiled in return as he parked. "Is this where we're having dinner? Because, Jaxx, you need a reservation here. You can't just walk in."

I held back a wince as I realized that he thought I had no idea how to live in his world, a world where everyone knew they had to make a reservation at a nice restaurant.

"We have a reservation." I started to walk toward the restaurant.

He slipped his arm around mine and glanced over at me. "You know it's not my birthday, right?"

"Yes." I laughed as we reached the door of the restaurant.

He paused and pulled me a little closer to him. "Are you going to tell me what this is all about now?" His fingertips coasted along the soft skin of my forearm before his hand wrapped around mine.

"I invited you to dinner, remember?" I licked my lips, forgetting that they were coated in lipstick and gloss. The taste made me wince.

"I remember." He stared into my eyes, his hand still tangled with mine. "Is that all you're going to tell me?"

"Nate, if you don't want to be here, I understand." My heart dropped as the words spilled out.

For a split-second every ounce of confidence I had vanished. What if I'd made a terrible mistake? What if I had ruined a fantastic friendship all on some crazy whim that he might just feel the same way about me?

"Of course I want to be here." He frowned as he gave my hand a light squeeze. "I'm exactly where I want to be."

His words set off a wave of warmth through me. Did he mean it? Or did he only say it to protect my feelings?

Just his light touch on my arm was enough to inspire that shower of sparks again. How had I missed this? How had I been so blind to how I felt about him?

I couldn't deny it, no matter the risk. I had to take my chance before it was too late.

TWENTY-EIGHT

As we settled at the table, my confidence began to falter again.

Yes, I knew how to make a reservation, but now I was out of my depth. The menu was extensive and without a price in sight. The other diners all seemed to know exactly what they wanted, how to order it, and how to behave in the fancy surroundings.

Me, on the other hand? I got the tablecloth caught under my thigh and had to catch my glass of water before it slid off the edge of the table.

My cheeks flushed as I tugged the tablecloth free.

"This is a great place." Nate smiled across the table at me.

"I thought you might like it." I smiled in return then tried to settle my pounding heart. All I had to do was make a good impression. Why did that feel so impossible?

"I come here a lot with my family." He shrugged as he settled back in his chair and picked up his menu.

I fiddled with mine. I had plenty of money saved up, but I began to wonder if I'd underestimated the cost of the restaurant. Without any prices to guide me—and several items that I couldn't dream of pronouncing or understanding—my heart fluttered. I'd brought him to the restaurant to make a good impression, but I wondered if I'd end up embarrassing myself instead.

"What do you usually get?" I peeked at him over the top of the menu.

"Steak—with a baked potato." He set his menu down and met my eyes.

"I don't see that on here." I looked away from him as I skimmed the menu again.

"That's because they give everything funny names to make it sound fancier." He grinned as he took my menu from me. "I can order for us, if you'd like."

I felt some relief but also a sharp disappointment. I wanted to prove that I could fit into his world, but I felt as if I was just proving that I could never belong.

"Thanks." I looked down at the tablecloth and tried to regain my confidence. I couldn't give up, not when he was the prize.

"Jaxx." His voice summoned my eyes to his. "This is a great surprise. Thanks for inviting me."

"You're welcome." I swallowed hard as he shifted in his chair and leaned closer to me across the table.

"It's nice that's it's just the two of us. Maybe we can talk about some things."

"Like what?" I fiddled with my glass of water and glanced away from him.

"Like Maby."

My heart lurched. Was he about to tell me that they had gotten together? That it wasn't okay for him to be out to dinner with me?

"What about her? She seems sweet." I shrugged and forced myself to look back in his direction. I hoped that the waitress would show up to take our order before he could shatter my chances of being with him.

"I know you told me to give her a chance." He lowered his eyes for a moment, then looked back up at me. "But I just don't feel that way about her. I made it clear to her last night. I really value her friendship, but that's all we are—friends."

As relieved as I felt to hear it, I couldn't help but wonder if he was preparing to give me the same speech. Of course I knew that I was interested in him. I'd dressed up, put on make-up, invited him to a fancy dinner. He had to suspect that I was up to something.

I braced myself for the next words he would say.

But instead of speaking he just stared at me.

"That's good." I bit into my bottom lip, then shook my head. "I mean, if that's how you really feel. It's good that you told her the truth."

"You're right." He lowered his voice. "It wasn't easy. Admitting how you really feel isn't always easy. But I'm glad I did. She and I are still friends. It can be scary to risk that friendship, but you can't deny how you feel."

"No, I guess you can't." I felt his eyes search mine. I could sense that he wanted me to say something more.

Did he want me to admit the reason I'd invited him to dinner?

I reached for my glass of water again and knocked my fork off the table and onto the floor. "Oops." I reached for it, but a waitress swept in and grabbed it before I could touch it.

"Don't worry, I'll get you another." She eyed me for a moment, then turned and walked away.

My cheeks grew hot. I could barely take a breath. Why did I have to be such a disaster? I couldn't pretend to be something I wasn't. As much as I wanted to be with Nate, I wasn't ever going to feel comfortable at a fancy restaurant.

"Sorry." I mumbled as I avoided his eyes.

"Jaxx." He sighed as he reached across the table and took my hand again. "Why are we here?"

"For dinner." My throat felt dry as I met his eyes.

His lips twitched somewhere between a smile and a frown as he sighed again. "So you keep saying. You know you can tell me anything, right?"

My heart skipped a beat as I continued to stare into his eyes. In that moment I believed him. But telling him the truth didn't mean that he would feel the same way about me.

"We should probably order." I glanced around for our waitress.

"Jaxx." He squeezed my hand.

I looked back at him. The moment I met his eyes, he smiled.

"Do you trust me?"

The question struck me as strange, but the answer was easy.

"Yes." I trusted him more than he could possibly know. I trusted that he would never hurt me. I trusted that he would always rescue me from the waves—of the ocean and my crazy emotions.

"Great." He stood up from the table, then pulled me to my feet. "Let's go."

TWENTY-NINE

Nate whisked me out of the restaurant before the waitress could even make it over to us.

As he started the jeep, I sank down in my seat. I felt as if I'd failed at everything. I had picked the right restaurant, worn the right clothes and make-up, but I still couldn't get through a single meal in Nate's world.

Had I embarrassed him so much that he couldn't stand to be there a moment longer?

He turned the radio up as it played one of our favorite songs. As he hummed along, he rolled the windows down.

I started to smooth down my hair, afraid to have it ruffled by the wind, but a second later I let it fly.

He glanced over at me and smiled. "Isn't this better?"

I stared at him for a long moment. "I'm sorry, Nate."

"Sorry?" He pulled to a stop in front of a food truck near the beach. "For what?"

"I wanted things to be different tonight." I looked down at my folded hands settled against the dress that I didn't belong in and sighed.

"Things *will* be different." He leaned close to me. "At least,

I hope they will be. Pepperoni, right?" He hopped out of the jeep and jogged over to the food truck.

I watched him order slices of my favorite pizza and felt some comfort. Even if things hadn't gone as planned at least I would have a nice evening with him.

Would I still be brave enough to confess my feelings?

He opened my door and held his hand out to me. "Will you join me for dinner?"

"That's supposed to be my line tonight." I smiled as I took his hand and stepped out of the jeep.

"I'm glad you invited me." He led me toward the beach. "But you didn't seem very comfortable."

I slid my heels off as we stepped into the sand. "You noticed?" My cheeks warmed as I looked out over the water.

"I noticed a lot of things." He pulled me closer to him as we walked across the beach. "Your hair. Your make-up." He turned to face me. "I've never seen you like this before."

"That was kind of the point." I dug my toes into the sand and bit into my bottom lip.

His eyes lingered on me as if he was waiting for me to say something more, but I couldn't bring myself to speak a single word.

"Jaxx." He tipped his head toward mine so that our faces were only inches apart, and we shared the same salty air.

"I'm sorry, Nate." As soon as I whispered the words, my heart raced and emotions rushed to the surface. "I know all of this must seem strange to you. I know it doesn't make any sense. I just thought that if you saw me this way—if I could look more like Maby—like Kelsie—or if I could eat at a fancy restaurant, I just thought...well, maybe..." My throat tightened before I could finish.

"Maybe what?" He set the pizza box down on the sand beside us, then settled his hands on my shoulders as he looked back at me. "No more avoiding it. You've had something to say since this night started and I've been waiting to hear it. So, tell me the truth, Jaxx. Why are we here?"

I could barely draw a breath as he stared into my eyes. This was it. This was the moment when I had to admit that I didn't think I could ever go back to being his friend, that I doubted that I would ever stop wanting to be with him. It could be the moment that our friendship ended once and for all, or it could be the moment when everything changed between us. But all of it depended on my being able to speak.

I felt his warm palms curve around my shoulders and the reassuring grasp of his fingertips as he held me in place. Did he think I might run?

It did cross my mind.

"I'll never be like them, Nate." My voice trembled as I spoke. I heard the fear in it and did my best to infuse confidence into my next words. "I don't want to be like them. If that's what you want, then I understand."

"I'd never want you to be like them either." A breeze fluttered between us, sending my loose hair in a curtain across my face. He lifted his hands from my shoulders and swept them back through my hair. He tucked it behind my ears, then cradled the back of my neck as he looked into my eyes. "You look amazing, Jaxx, but you look amazing to me every single day. You have ever since the first day I saw you. I don't need you to be anything but yourself. I don't want you to be anyone other than you." He stepped closer to me, his forehead nearly touching mine as he spoke softly. "I've been waiting all night for you to say it. So please, just say it."

"Nate, I don't want to be your friend." My heart pounded. "I mean, I do. I love being your friend. But I want more than that. But I want that too and if that's all I can have, then I'll take it. I mean, I'll be glad to have it. I get it, I'm not like other girls and I know that you would never want to hurt my feelings and I've put you in this awkward position..."

"Jaxx." He smiled as he said my name, then swept me into a passionate kiss.

The sand disappeared beneath me, not because the waves swept it away, but because I felt as if I'd begun to float. With just a single kiss, everything had changed.

As he pulled away from me, I felt that sensation again—as if the current was tugging at me—only this time it tugged me right toward him.

"I'm so glad you finally said it. But that doesn't mean I won't eat all the pizza." He grabbed the box from the ground and took off at a sprint across the beach.

"Hey! Don't eat my pepperoni!" I laughed as I chased after him.

THIRTY

Over the next few weeks, I spent almost every free moment I had with Nate. I learned to surf, to dance, and to kiss in a way that I'd never even known was a possibility. I tried to savor every moment that we had together.

Both Kelsie and I had accepted offers to continue working for the two families in the city after the summer was over. This was exciting to me for many reasons, including the possibility of continued time spent with Nate.

A spray of sand hit me right in the face as Bella ran toward the water.

"Wait up, little one!" I laughed as I chased after her. I sent a quick glance toward the lifeguard stand where Nate sat, his eyes on the water.

"Bella! Let's go, lunch time!" Hannah called out to her as she gathered the other kids up. "Let's let Jaxx and Kelsie have a little quiet time."

Kelsie walked over to me, then sighed as she glanced in the direction of a group of guys further down the beach.

"I'm going to break things off with Lance. I've been putting it off, but it has to be done."

"Are you sure?" I frowned. "I thought you kind of liked him?"

"Kind of." She shrugged. "But to be honest, after what I've seen between you and Nate—well, I get it now."

"Get what?" I met her eyes.

"Why you waited. It's different, different than anything I've ever experienced. So far, the summer hasn't started out with any love connections for me, but who knows what will happen next?" She smiled as she walked off in Lance's direction.

I couldn't help but smile at her description of my relationship with Nate. She wasn't wrong. It did feel a bit like a fairytale. It felt like everything I'd been waiting for and nothing I'd ever known before.

Nate climbed down from the lifeguard stand as Frankie took over.

"Hey, beautiful." He grinned as he wrapped his arms around me. "I've been counting down the minutes until my break."

"Me too." I smiled.

As he leaned in to kiss me, I caught sight of Maby walking toward us. I pulled away from the kiss, a little flustered by the thought of her seeing it. She had made herself fairly scarce around us lately.

"Well, well, if it isn't the lovebirds." She laughed as she crossed her arms. "Go on, I don't want to interrupt anything."

"It's alright." I took a step back from Nate.

"Jaxx." Maby met my eyes. "Really, it's fine. Nate was right. We work best as friends. But now he needs to step up and do the right thing by his friend."

"What's that?" I felt some relief as Maby wrapped an arm around each of us.

"He needs to hook me up with one of his friends." Maby

grinned, then winked at Nate. "And not Frankie!" She held up a hand as Nate looked up at the lifeguard stand. "Never Frankie!"

"He's really a sweet guy." Nate laughed.

"Did I ask for sweet?" She raised her eyebrows. "Anyway, I know it'll be hard to resist, but Jaxx, you've got to get him focused on this task. Alright?"

"I'll do my best." I looked over at Nate.

"Nope, sorry, I'm already distracted." Nate pulled me close and kissed me.

I laughed as we broke apart again. "I'm sure it can't be hard to find someone for Maby."

"Oh no, not hard at all." He looked over at her. "Guys line up for a chance to date you. But the problem is, you're picky."

"Well, they can't all be you, Nate." Maby shrugged. "It's not my fault you don't have a brother."

"She has a point." I nodded as I gave Nate a stern look. "Why don't you have a nice brother?"

"I guess you'd have to ask my mother that question." He laughed, then shook his head. "Don't worry, there's no doubt in my mind that your Mr. Perfect is out there just waiting for you."

"Well, he's taking his sweet time." She fluffed her hair, then marched off in Kelsie's direction.

As I watched Maby and Kelsie meet up near the waves, I knew how lucky I was to have found Nate—to have fought for him and to have been brave enough to admit my true feelings, even when it felt impossible to do so.

"How about a swim?" Nate grabbed my hand and pulled me toward the water.

"Race you!" I grinned as I shook my hand free and took off ahead of him.

I'd expected a lot from my summer in the Hamptons—a great adventure away from home—but never in my wildest dreams could I have imagined that I'd find such happiness with a guy like Nate.

ALSO BY JILLIAN ADAMS

Amazon.com/author/jillianadams

NANNY TALES: THE HAMPTONS SERIES

It Started With A Rescue (Jaxx and Nate)

It Started With A Joke (Kelsie and Frankie)

It Started With A Song (Maby and Devon)

OAK BROOK ACADEMY SERIES

The New Girl (Sophie and Wes)

Falling for Him (Alana and Mick)

No More Hiding (Apple and Ty)

Worth the Wait (Maby and Oliver)

A Fresh Start (Jennifer and Gabriel)

Taking a Chance (Candy and Nicholas)

Risking it All (Savannah and Ethan)

Time for Healing (Lily and Austin)

Made in the USA
Monee, IL
12 December 2021

85062808R00080